HUT   HAR   TO   ...

Hampshire County Council
www.hants.gov.uk/lib
0845

KT-465-908

The Granton Gang

Bluff Point was a peaceful town where nothing ever happened – until the Granton gang raided the bank. But their carefully laid plans were a wasted effort when the crafty bank manager and town preacher interfered.

After a shoot-out the town seemed able to settle down again. But, during the attempted heist, Alf Granton had stumbled upon information that could make him rich. The town was covering up for a past crime and Alf knew just who was responsible.

It all led to more killings and a final shoot-out with the Grantons that brought about a surprise and bloody ending.

The Granton Gang

Tom Benson

A Black Horse Western

ROBERT HALE · LONDON

© Tom Benson 2005
First published in Great Britain 2005

ISBN 0 7090 7823 4

Robert Hale Limited
Clerkenwell House
Clerkenwell Green
London EC1R 0HT

The right of Tom Benson to be identified as
author of this work has been asserted by him
in accordance with the Copyright, Designs and
Patents Act 1988.

HAMPSHIRE COUNTY LIBRARY	
C013913974	
HJ	02/02/2006
F	£10.99
0709078234	

Typeset by
Associates, Shaw Heath.
bound in Great Britain by
ve Limited, Wiltshire

ONE

The wagon was drawn by a couple of large mules and there were two men up on the seat as it moved smartly along the trail towards the lumber camp. Two other men accompanied it, riding small cowponies and armed with shotguns and revolvers. There were provisions on the rig: food and coffee-beans, with bundles of blankets amid a collection of kegs containing lamp-oil, molasses, and everything else needed to keep the lumber camp going for another month.

There was something else in the wagon, which was buried beneath the innocent cargo. A linen bag carried the payroll. It was not a lot of money but there were almost a hundred men to be paid and it amounted to the best part of $2,000 in small notes and coins. It had come from the bank in Bluff Point and the man who sat next to the driver

always used the supply rig as a cover for the trans-
action.

Max Easton was a big man, running to fat, with
a red face and bulbous nose above a straggly moustache which was greying around the dark edges.
He sat with a shotgun across his knee, intent on his
need to get the payroll safely through and demonstrate his efficiency to the bosses who controlled
his life.

The first part of the journey out of town was easy
enough. The trail was flat and with few trees or
bushes that could hide a hold-up gang. It was the
next part that always worried him. The ground
dipped into a sandy waste for several miles and
then the two buttes came into sight. They were tall
outcrops of rock that ran parallel to each other
like a deep gorge before opening out on higher
ground where the tree-line reared along the edges
of the distant hills.

The camp moved closer to the hills each season
as more trees were felled and the ground became
an open space. The topsoil was falling away in the
rains to leave a gritty mess that would only grow
mesquite and tall cactus plants which stood like
sentries along the route the wagon was taking.

They had to travel between the two buttes which
towered on either side like solid towers of red
stone. The sound of the wheels echoed in the
confined space and the men on the rig eyed every

stone and hollow with unease. The two others on their horses were equally alert as they went through the shadowed walls of rock. It was at the far end, when the open highland lay before them, that it happened.

The way was barred by a row of large stones which were piled across the trail from wall to wall of the gorge. It was not a high barrier; just a couple of feet or less. But a wagon could not pass, and the men would have to get down to remove the stones before they could go further. The driver pulled the rig to a halt and all four men looked fearfully around at the menacing position in which they found themselves.

Their guns were cocked and the big man in charge was scanning the space in case the rig could be turned back. There was not enough room to bring the mules round and he bit his lip angrily before shouting to the two horsemen.

'Cover me while I move those rocks,' he bawled. 'And shoot anythin' that moves around here. I ain't aimin' to be vulture meat.'

He got down from the rig, leaving his shotgun on the seat as he edged his way carefully towards the barrier. The rocks were easy to move. Each one was not more than the weight of a new-born calf. Max Eaton was sweating as he moved the first few stones and flung them angrily to the side of the trail. His eyes were darting backwards and forwards among the bushes and fissures of the butte walls. The place was almost like a canyon and he would never have used it but for the worn trail which would take the rig easily in normal circumstances.

He was cursing as he picked up another piece of stone. Then a volley of shots rang out, scaring up the birds and echoing around the walls of reddish rock.

The big man fell to his knees; a bullet had entered his left thigh and he struggled to crawl for shelter beneath the rig. The driver was already on the ground. His face was disfigured from a shot that had hit him in the cheek and left him unconscious on the bloodstained earth.

The two horsemen had quickly dismounted. One was slightly injured as they both ran for whatever cover the ground could give them. Their animals were spooked by the noise and galloped back the way they had come, to vanish from sight. The shooting was coming from several points amid the rocks. A blast from a shotgun hit one of the mules and it reared up before staggering against its terrified companion and collapsing.

The young horseman, who was not injured, crawled beneath the rig to join his boss.

'They've got us trapped here, Mr Eaton,' he quavered. 'Throw them the money and let's get the hell out.'

'You gotta be jokin', lad, or you gotta be one lily-livered pantywaist. I fought in the war without turnin' tail, and I don't aim to start now. Just pick out where the shots are comin' from and pin 'em down.'

The big man knelt behind a wheel and aimed his pistol at a clump of rocks. He fired with a steady hand despite the pain in his leg, and swore vividly as chips flew off the sandstone instead of finding a better target. The young man fired in the same direction. His hand was shaking as he emptied the Lefaucheaux pistol furiously before having to start pushing the ejector to reload. A shot took the other mule and it thrashed around dangerously as it dragged the rig backwards and forwards.

The wheel against which the big man was kneeling began to move erratically and he slipped as it hit him. Amid a flock of new curses, he opened fire again while the young man at his side flattened himself to the ground. A bullet sprayed his head with gravel. Another tore splinters from the wagon above him.

'I reckon there's five or six of them,' Max Eaton said as he reloaded his .44. 'They're all at one end of the trail but we got no mules to make a getaway. I'm hurt bad, Joe's dead, and Ray seems to have his own troubles back there. You're the only one with two sound legs, lad. You gotta make a run for it.'

'On foot?'

'Sure, why not? Ray and me can still hold 'em off and it's a cinch that their horses are somewhere near them. They gotta get past us to chase you. Once you're clear of this gorge, there's plenty of scrub out there and they'll never find you. Are you game?'

The younger man thought it over for a moment.

'I reckon there ain't a lot of choice,' he said quietly. 'But what about you and Ray?'

'They'll kill us anyways, lad. That's the way of these folk. But I don't aim they should have the payroll as well. You take that, make your way due north, but keep off the trail until you're sure you're clear of any followers. You'll be mighty welcome back at the camp, and I figure as you'll be havin' free drinks for a week. Now hoist yourself on to the back of the rig without gettin' a bullet in your ass, grab that bag of cash under the molasses barrels, and high-tail it outa here. I'll get closer to Ray and we'll keep up a good rate of fire while you're doin' it.'

'You'll get killed, sure as shootin' if you don't go with me,' the young man said desperately.

'I can't move far with this leg, son, and neither can Ray. You're the only one with a chance, and I aim to disappoint them fellas when all they find on the rig is a load of foodstuffs that ain't worth a damn. Now, get goin' while you can.'

The young man crawled under the wagon

towards the front where one mule was lying dead and the other still thrashed around. He came up against the shaft and hauled himself over the driver's seat and down among the barrels and sacks. The canvas bag of cash was easy to find and he dropped it to the ground before slipping back himself. The dying mule nearly kicked him as he recovered the money and moved back to Max Eaton's side.

The big man gave him a weak grin.

'Good work, son,' he muttered. 'Now get on your way and lose yourself in the scrub once you're on the high ground. I reckon we can hold them off another half hour or so. Then it's up to you. Your best plan is to lie low as near here as possible. They'll go harin' out after you, thinkin' you're headin' straight for the camp. They won't reckon on you stayin' right near the place where all the shootin' was happening. Go on. Get yourself outa here.'

The young man nodded dumbly and began to crawl along the trail. He could hear the increased firing behind him as he sweated his way past the mules to edge closer to the boulders that blocked the route out of the gorge. He got through the space where Max Eaton had moved a few of the rocks. It was easier after that. He could not be seen from the far end of the gorge and no shots came in his direction.

11

It took him ten minutes of dodging and weaving among the bushes and stones before he was on the clear upper part of the trail. He straightened up and looked around at the vast empty space with the myriad clusters of mesquite, thorn-bushes, and tall, sentrylike cactus plants. He knew that Max was right about what to do next. He turned to his left, pushed his way through a mass of dust-covered bushes, and found a space where he could lie down, and where nobody would be likely to find him.

He was tired and thirsty, his limbs trembling with fatigue and fear as he tucked the bag into the middle of a thorn-bush and lay silently while he listened to the shooting which still echoed from the gorge.

It suddenly stopped and the noises of the birds and myriad insects became noticeable again. The young man listened carefully but no more shots were fired. He lay flat on the ground, pulling some brushwood around himself and hoping that when the hold-up men broke out of the gorge they would pass him by.

Half an hour or more elapsed and the sun was at its peak as it beat down relentlessly on the hidden fugitive. He was almost dazed by the suffocating heat and the sharp smells of the plants. His eyes flickered as he heard a sudden strange noise that was like the beat of a drum. It was the sound of horses, moving somewhere close by and echoing through the ground where he lay.

He licked his lips nervously and hardly drew breath when the sound became a hard reality as a troop of horsemen careered through the grassland and sped on to the north without even pausing to search an area so close to the killings. The young man breathed a deep sigh of relief as the hoof-beats receded and the noises of the natural world took over again.

He lay back with a smile of content on his face and a tiredness overcame him despite the heat. He drifted off into a deep sleep and did not wake until the sun was past its peak and a cool wind trembled the grasses around him.

After recovering the bag of money, he got to his feet and stood uncertainly. There was a compulsion to go back to the gorge and see what had happened. But they would all be dead, and it was not a place to be trapped.

Max had told him to head north, and he knew that if he kept parallel to the trail he would eventually reach the lumber camp in the foothills. And he would be a hero when he got there.

The young man started out, but he had plans of his own and was heading due east.

TWO

Bluff Point was a quiet little town with one saloon, a main street of small stores, and a meeting-house next to the burial plot where the faithful met every Sunday and sang their hearts out to the music of Mr Moody and Mr Sankey. The jailhouse was halfway down the main street, next to the bank but looking more dilapidated and not catering for the same prosperous type of customer.

The marshal liked Bluff Point. His biggest headache was the occasional drunk or the spooking of a horse, which would excite all the small boys to whoops and hollering while everybody tried to control the animal. Ethan Welsby had been the lawman for fourteen years and intended to stay on until old age forced him to retire to the little cabin where he and his equally stout wife lived in plain but happy surroundings.

He never turned up at the jailhouse until about ten each morning. It seemed a reasonable hour and nobody ever bothered him about it. But there was something different today. A flurry of excitement seemed to be upsetting the folks on the main street and they were beginning to gather around the hardware store opposite his own place of work. The mayor owned the large wooden building and was standing in the doorway, talking to the people and waving his hands furiously to make his point. Whatever it was.

Marshal Welsby bit his lip angrily. If the lanky, pale-faced mayor was flustered and beseiged by angry townsfolk, then it could spell trouble. He hurried gown the street and mounted the stoop to ask Jess Bradley what was happening.

'Happening!' the mayor yelled at him. ''We've got no damned water! That's what's happening. And where the hell have you been?'

Ethan looked flustered for a moment and then recovered himself enough to put up a defence.

'My well ain't dried up,' he protested. 'And there was rain last week fit to drown a herd of steers. We can't be short of water.'

There was shouting from the crowd as everyone tried to speak at once. Their fists were raised and some of the women had parasols that looked more dangerous than the guns at the waists of their menfolk.

'Your well is deep water, Ethan,' the mayor explained impatiently. 'It's the creek. The town has to have the creek flowin' or we're in trouble. What you figurin' on doin' about it?'

The marshal looked around in some puzzlement. It was going to be a hot day and the idea of following the course of the creek until the blockage was found did not appeal to him.

'I'll send young Jim Clark with a coupla helpers,' he said with sudden decision. 'They can trace back until they find out what's gone wrong. We'll have it right in no time.'

The scrawny mayor gripped the marshal's elbow with surprising strength.

'You'll go yourself,' Jess Bradley snarled, 'and leave the young fella to look after the town. I want to see the marshal at the head of what's happenin' around here. Get some buckboards, plenty of shovels and blastin' powder, and get your ass along the line of that goddamned creek.'

The marshal nodded glumly and turned to the crowd of men who stood around chuntering angrily among themselves. He soon mustered volunteers, the livery stable owner went to get the buckboard, and everything was set to go.

The mayor looked pleased with himself. He had shown true leadership and would accompany the expedition to demonstrate that the First Citizen was a real man of the people. The fact that an election was only a year away might also have influenced his decision. He was not even plagued by the usual demand for money from the volunteers. They all knew that this was something they had to do in their own interests. The fast-flowing creek was vital. Except for the few deep wells at the southern end of town, all the water supply came from it.

It was the very reason that Bluff Point had been built on that particular spot. A good flow of clear water ran down from the distant hills. It was filtered through sand and pebble-beds and was sweet to the taste and always reliable. Until now.

Mayor Bradley went back into the hardware store and collected his hat to go saddle the fat old mare that carried him gently around town. He was already having second thoughts about his decision, but the idea of the election drove him on and he was at the head of the procession that set out an hour later towards the north, travelling along the banks of the rapidly drying creek.

Bluff Point fell quiet as the dust-trailing expedition vanished from sight. People went back to their normal pursuits in the certainty that the water would start flowing again in a few hours.

Marshal Welsby's deputy leaned on the hitching rail outside the jailhouse. He was a young, gangling lad with light blond hair and slim hands that played with a small knife and a piece of wood. He was whittling something, but what it was nobody would ever know. It was simply a habit with

17

him. A way of keeping occupied by a young man who neither smoked nor chewed tobacco. His slim body was encased in a grey wool shirt and canvas pants that were worn but clean. He carried a Colt .44 at his belt but it had not been fired for months, and then only against a saguaro cactus that he used for target practice. Life was dull for a young fellow who wanted to be one of the famous marshals of the West like those mentioned in the *Dime Magazine.*

He sometimes thought that those days might be over and that he would just go on deputizing until old Ethan Welsby retired and left him the solitaire cards and leather chair behind the flat-topped desk. It was not a bad life but he itched for just a little more excitement now and then.

The main street was nearly deserted. The women were not yet out to do their shopping; the children were in the schoolroom, and only Preacher Swann was occupied in putting a piece of paper on the church notice-board. Jim Clark straightened up, put the knife back in his pocket and went into the jailhouse to make himself a cup of coffee.

That was why he missed the arrival of the Granton gang. They rode into town from both ends of the main street. Three came from the north and two from the south. They were lean-looking men on rough cow ponies, and each

18

carried a shotgun as well as pistols at his belt.

Alf Granton was in his fifties, dark-faced and with a mouth that was a straight line of determination. His eyes were pale blue, watering slightly from the dust but alert and keen as he surveyed the street and watched every move around him. His two sons were at his side. Phil and Tom were just younger versions of their father, with the same pale eyes and thin lips. Tom had a new and livid scar at the side of his mouth. He liked folks to think that it was earned in a fight, but the truth was more prosaic. A saloon girl had hit him with a bottle. The two brothers were in their early twenties and tufts of dark hair stuck out from under their hats as they rode towards the bank.

Few glances were thrown at them in the quiet street. Only a couple of elderly men paid attention as they chatted to each other in front of the Lady Luck saloon and waited for it to open.

The five horsemen came to a halt outside the bank, dismounted and hitched their animals before gathering in a little knot in front of the glass-panelled door. The two other members of the gang were older than Alf Granton's sons. They had mean, pinched faces and had not shaved for weeks. At a nod from Alf, they all entered together, drawing their guns as they did so.

There were six customers at the counter, all of them local business men who were preparing for the day's transactions in their various stores. Everybody looked round in surprise and hardly a word was said as they all raised their hands and paled at the sight of the guns. Some coins fell to the floor with a loud rattle as a trembling hand lost its grip.

'Now, don't go gettin' no silly ideas, fellas, and nobody gets hurt,' Alf Granton said calmly. 'Just stay put while me and the lads collect a few dollars for comfort in our old age.'

He motioned to his companions and they acted with experienced speed. One guarded the door, while another climbed over the counter and began gathering up all the available cash into a canvas bag which he drew from under his shirt.

Another young fellow began relieving the customers of their watches and tie-pins. Alf went straight through to the office in the rear and found a man in shirt-sleeves bent over a ledger at the manager's desk. He looked like an elderly clerk and stared in dumb puzzlement at the intruder.

The safe was a tall green-painted thing in the far corner. It was shut and there was no key in the lock.

'Open it up and be quick about it,' Alf Granton ordered as he waved his gun.

The elderly man shook his head.

'I ain't got the keys,' he stuttered. 'Mr Cullen

took them with him.'

Alf Granton cursed and looked wildly round the office. 'And where the hell is he?' he demanded.

The clerk waved his arms about as if in explanation.

'It's the creek,' he tried to explain. 'It's dried up and they've all ridden out to see what caused it. Mr Cullen went with them.'

Alf Granton swore luridly and banged a fist against the door of the safe. He motioned the clerk to join the others in the main part of the bank and followed him angrily with his gun poking the man in the small of the back.

The others had finished their work and looked surprised at seeing the boss coming out of the office without a bag of money. He told them what had happened in as few words as possible and looked round for inspiration.

'Let's get the hell out,' he snarled, 'and make sure these fellas ain't left with nothin' worth having.'

Tom grinned. 'I got their guns, Pa,' he said, 'and some nice stick-pins.'

'Good lad. Now let's start movin' before the town wakes up.'

They hurried out of the building and made for their horses. They were just about to mount when the window of the bank suddenly shattered with a deafening noise that was enough to alert the whole street. Someone had pitched a chair through the painted glass.

It woke Jim Clark from his doze in the jailhouse and he jumped to his feet in alarm. A glance from the window was enough to tell him what was happening. He grabbed a shotgun from the rack and checked its load as he made for the door. He saw a group of horsemen leaving the bank and heading away from him as they gathered pace to reach the edge of town.

He let fly with both barrels, but the range was too great to be really effective. He drew his Colt and fired a couple of shots as the bandits turned the corner into one of the side lanes. A horse stumbled but recovered enough to take its rider out of sight.

Another man was running from the southern end of the main street. It was the preacher and he carried a Winchester which he was loading as he ran towards the turn-off where the horsemen had now disappeared. As the deputy watched helplessly, the preacher stopped at the entrance to the narrow side lane and coolly raised the gun to his shoulder. He fired a rapid volley of shots and then silently stood shaking his head as though in disbelief in his own actions.

When Jim Clark caught up with him and was able to see down the lane, he was confronted by two dead horses and one apparently dead bank robber. Another one lay trapped under his animal and was struggling to free himself. The deputy ran down the rutted lane and took the man's guns before hauling him from under the cowpony and handing him over to the few men who had now gathered to help the lawman.

The preacher still stood at the junction with the main street. He looked rather shocked at what he had done and the Winchester was held limply in his right hand. The reverend Richard Swann was a man in his middle forties. He was tall, well built, and with pale skin that seemed stretched across the facial bones. His dark eyes were always compassionate and he was a loved preacher who had a large congregation, even from among those who would normally have not gone anywhere near a church meeting.

Bluff Point was a lucky town to have a preacher who did not threaten the fires of eternal damnation or rant against drink and gambling. He was a tolerant man, who simply led by example and had a wife who worked hard for the local people while she still had time to look after her husband and bring up two boys and a girl.

He stood without moving, even as the mortician and the doctor arrived to push past him in their eagerness to get at the scene and earn a few dollars. The surviving bank robber was already being marched off towards the jailhouse and the young deputy was picking up the guns that lay in the dust.

'I've never killed a man,' the preacher said in a flat voice to nobody in particular. 'I only meant to stop them. I really did.'

The medical man heard the words and got up from his knees.

He was short and fat with a large moustache that joined his sideburns across tanned cheeks.

'You ain't killed nobody, Preacher,' Doc Porter assured him. 'He hit his head when he came off the horse, so maybe the animal kicked him. He'll come round in a few minutes and face trial with the other fella.'

The preacher's face cleared and he grasped the rifle with more confidence.

'I thought I couldn't be that bad a shot,' he said thankfully. 'Well, I'll get back to my work. Unless the folk in the bank need any help.'

'The only thing they need is to get their money back,' the doctor said drily.

Jim Clark was now on his way to the bank. People were crowding around and the town seemed suddenly alive as agitated women and elderly men pestered him for information he did not have. The bank clerks were at the door, brushing off the complaints of customers and taking a small pride in the fact that the robbers had got so little.

The elderly clerk who had been in the manager's office was inside the building. He looked different now. His figure was more upright; he wore an expensive frock-coat and a gold watch-chain spread itself across his stomach. George Cullen had resumed his role as bank manager and was in his office, waiting for the deputy's appearance.

'Did they get much, Mr Cullen?' Jim asked anxiously.

The man shook his head and smiled with modest bravery.

'No, they did not,' he said cheerfully. 'As soon as I heard the ruckus out front, I locked the safe, took off my coat, and posed as a clerk. Told them that the manager had gone out of town with the others. All they got was the three hundred dollars that I had on my desk.'

He spoke without a blush as he threw open the safe door and showed the contents to the lawman.

'Fourteen thousand dollars in there,' he said proudly. 'And all they made off with was four hundred and twenty dollars all told. Plus the watches and guns of the customers. Quick thinking. That's what it's all about, Deputy.'

'You sure did well, Mr Cullen. And did you throw the chair through the window?'

'I did indeed. Had to wake up the town some-how. Fred Stales tells me that you have two of

25

them. Any money recovered?' Jim Clark shook his head.

'I don't think so,' he admitted. 'There was a fella with a bag across his saddle, but the two we've got here don't seem to have anything. I'm goin' to the jailhouse now to ask a few questions.'

The bank manager's cheek showed a slight tic as he thought about his own story.

'The fella that came into my office,' he said, 'was an older man than the others seem to have been. I reckon he was the boss. And he sure acted strangely. Shoved the notes I had on the desk straight into his shirt. I reckon as how he wasn't goin' to share with the others.'

'Well, I'll try and get somethin' outa the two we have, Mr Cullen. I'll leave you to clear up now.'

'Are you goin' after them, lad?'

Jim shook his head.

'No, I got no men young enough for a posse and they've had too much of a start on us. I figure that the two we've got might start talkin' if we ask questions the right way. There's bound to be a hideout some place.'

The manager nodded agreement but added a note of warning.

'Just don't let Judge Lawson catch you usin' any rough stuff, lad,' he advised. 'He's one of them folks who's all for doin' things legal. Gets justice and law mixed up, so he does.'

Jim Clark nodded thanks for the advice and left on his errand while George Cullen poured himself a glass of whiskey and patted the $300 that lay in his pocket.

THREE

The mayor's office was thick with smoke as he and the councilmen sat around and discussed what had happened in their town. The cheapest whiskey had been handed out to show that the First Citizen was in no mood to be hospitable. His tall, thin frame dominated from behind the flat-topped desk round which they sat.

Only the marshal and his deputy were left standing, defining their positions as employees rather than part of the ruling body of Bluff Point. And young Jim Clark had not even been offered a glass of whiskey.

'Well, we was taken for a real bunch of rubes,' the mayor said bitterly as he looked around. 'These fellas dam the creek with rocks, get all the able-bodied men outa Bluff Point, and then raid the bank. It was well thought out, and we was lucky not to come out worse than we did. George Cullen here did some mighty quick thinkin' and we're one fortunate town. So, now we gotta see what can be done about this.'

He waved his tumbler of whiskey at the marshal.

'What have them two fellas told you, Ethan?' he asked. 'Have you made them talk yet?'

Marshal Welsby glanced at the old judge who sat looking at his whiskey glass. Disgust was clearly written on his wrinkled face.

'I'm still workin' on them, Mayor,' he said slowly. 'They're mighty stubborn fellas, but I reckon they'll tell us who they are and where they hide out sooner or later.'

'Well, I'd rather it was sooner,' the mayor snapped. 'Give the bastards a good leatherin' and leave 'em without food for a few hours. That'll make 'em talk.'

The judge appeared to come out of his hostile trance.

'Ain't legal,' he wheezed. 'You gotta treat folk proper these days or their lawyers will have a reason for stoppin' the trial.'

'We only have one lawyer in this town,' the mayor retorted, 'and Harry ain't in the mood to stop any trial. He lost his watch and chain in that bank.'

'And my gun,' Lawyer Dettmold said bitterly.

'What the hell does a lawyer need a gun for?' one of the councilmen asked tartly.

'We got enemies,' he was told with a massive

29

glare. 'Lawyers ain't the most popular folk.'

'Ain't that the truth?' the marshal muttered to his deputy.

'Well, I say we gotta do everything legal,' the judge insisted. 'If we don't obey all these new-fangled laws, the Washington crowd will be down on us *muy pronto*, and then some. And I aim to keep this job until the preacher starts reading my eulogy.'

His remark lightened the atmosphere a little and it was the loud coughing of Councilman Hutton that drew attention to the fact that he had something to say. He was a big man who ran the livery stable and was reckoned to be one of the smarter people in town. Local folk tended to say that he was so big that his stomach arrived on the scene several minutes before he did. All eyes turned on him now while the judge went back to looking angrily at the whiskey in his glass.

'I reckon the marshal should go back to the jail-house,' Steve Hutton said, 'and ask 'em all polite-like to tell us who they are and where their hideout is. If they won't talk, then it could just be that he'll have to use other methods.'

'That's just what I've been saying, Steve,' the mayor cut in.

'But you was suggestin' violence,' the livery-stable owner said with a wink, 'and the judge won't have that sorta thing. There's an easier way, and not a finger gets laid on their delicate hides.'

*

The lamps were lit in the jailhouse and the two prisoners shared the only cell. A local drunk had been thrown out to make room for them and he had left protesting his rights to a night of board and lodging at the expense of the town. The marshal had given him a friendly boot in the pants that propelled him in the general direction of the saloon.

Marshal Welsby stood in front of the bars and looked at his captives with a grin on his round, tanned face. Jim Clark stood just behind him, holding a cup of coffee and waiting to see the fun.

'I got me some questions to ask you fellas before we put you in front of the judge tomorrow,' he said in an official voice. 'I want to know who you are, the names of the other three no-goods, and where in hell they're hidin' out right now.'

The two men came across to the bars and stared at the lawman as though they did not understand what he was saying. Both were middle-aged with thin, worn faces and a heavy growth of beard. One had a gash at the side of his head where he had fallen from his mount and been thought dead by the preacher. He was the spokesman.

'We don't talk to strange fellas,' he said bluntly. 'I reckon as how you aim to send us to the territory

31

prison anyways, so why the hell should we give you the time of day?'

'Could lighten your sentence.'

The prisoner gave a wide, mirthless grin that showed yellow teeth.

'I reckon we'll just take what comes,' he said. The other man nodded silently.

Marshal Welsby winked at his deputy.

'You may have the right of it there,' he said slowly. 'I personally don't think we have much of a case against you two fellas though. We'll probably have to turn you loose unless you confess.'

The two men had just been turning to go sit on their bunks, but the marshal's words brought them to a halt. They came back to the bars and stared at him in disbelief.

'You sure got funny ideas, Marshal,' the one with the scar said quietly. 'We just get on our horses and ride outa town? Is that it?'

'That's it. Y'see, fella, our judge is one hell of a man for all them legal niceties. Bein' a lawyer, he don't go for justice like most folk. He's all for evidence and proof. I been askin' around and the people who was in the bank can't say for certain that you was there. Then again, you was found on the ground after your horses was shot under you. The preacher and my deputy here didn't actually see you comin' outa the bank, so Reverend Swann could have shot the wrong fellas.'

He shook his head sadly and scratched the side of his unshaven face.

'It don't make sense to me,' he admitted, 'and if I had my way, I'd find you guilty as hell and send you off to the territory prison. But I ain't the judge, and old man Lawson is a real stickler for law. Without a confession, I'll just have to turn you loose. You can leave town in the morning.'

The marshal turned away and started clearing the papers off the desk ready for departing to his bed. Jim Clark poured the last of the coffee over the fire in the stove to dampen it down for the night. As Marshal Welsby reached up to blow out the oil-lamp, he stopped as though struck by a sudden thought.

'When you leave in the morning,' he said carefully, 'you'd better ride like hell. It's gonna be real dangerous out there.'

The two bandits looked at each other.

'What do you mean, Marshal?' the scarred one asked.

Ethan Welsby left the lamp and walked back to the cell bars. He leaned towards the two men as though about to whisper some great secret.

'Well, you see, it's like this, fellas,' he said quietly. 'The folk round here think we have the right men, and when I let you go, they're gonna be mighty sore. You gotta remember that we had one long ride out to that creek, spent the best part of an hour in the heat of the day clearin' all them rocks, and then a hard ride back home. That don't sweeten no tempers. The folks feel that somebody's gotta pay for all that trouble. It ain't so much the bank they're riled about, it's four or five hours of hard riding.'

The two men nodded their understanding and the younger of them licked his lips uneasily.

'We'll at least have our guns,' he said hopefully.

'Oh, sure. I gotta return them. But I can't have you shootin' up the town, so the bullets will be staying in my desk. You're just gonna have to ride like hell to avoid the lynchin' party. They'll be waitin', sure as shooting. They did with the last fella we turned loose. Hanged him from the livery stable loadin' beam, they did.'

He crossed back to the desk and blew out the lamp.

'Anyways, you don't have to worry about that till morning, so sleep on it, fellas.'

The marshal and his deputy left the jailhouse and the two prisoners heard the key turning in the lock of the outer door.

A quietness settled over the little town and only a few rats scampered between the buildings while bats flew overhead looking for whatever food was on the wing in the cool, still air. The moon was full and threw huge shadows as a coyote moved boldly down the main street to drink at the creek.

Something else moved as well, casting a bigger shadow between the buildings in the little lanes.

The figure stopped at the rear of the jailhouse and called softly to the men inside. They got up from their bunks and went across to the high window with a glimmer of hope on their faces.

A shot rang out. It was followed by two more in quick succession and the prisoners fell back as the stench of powder and spilled blood filled the cell.

A long silence seemed to fall over the darkened little town as even the creatures of the night ceased their movements while the echoes of the shots died away. Then lights began to appear at windows and wary heads peered out to see what had happened.

Ethan Welsby and his deputy reached the jail-house at about the same time. The fat marshal was still tugging at his braces while the gunbelt at his waist was slipping down because he had fastened it on too quickly.

'Where the hell did them shots come from, fella?' he yelled to his young colleague.

'Sure sounded like this end of town,' Jim Clark answered. 'I reckon it was some place behind the main street.'

'Ain't nobody shoutin' for help and I don't hear no horses,' the marshal complained. 'Some of the locals should know who was shootin' at this time of night.'

He looked around as people began to gather on the street. They felt safer when the lawmen were about and one elderly woman pointed to the little lane that ran between the bank and the jailhouse. Marshal Welsby led the way fearfully down the rutted alley until he stood beneath the barred window of the jail. He looked around carefully, guided by lights that now shone from the windows and doorways of the neighbours.

'Well, there sure ain't anyone dyin' around here,' he said with a feeling of relief. 'I reckon it coulda been some drunk.'

The mayor and a few other prominent citizens had now arrived on the scene and people were beginning to wander freely around the area. Nobody could see any sign of trouble, and gradually, the marshal's view was accepted and folk started to go back to their homes. The lawmen returned to the main street and entered their own office. The mayor accompanied them, knowing that there was a bottle of whiskey in the old desk and that Marshal Welsby would need to steady his nerves.

Jim Clark struck a vesta to light the lamp, but paused in the middle of the act. They could all smell the powder and see the smoke haze in the glimmering light. They could also see the two dead men in the cell.

'Well, that sure as hell stops us catchin' up with

the rest of that goddamned gang,' the marshal murmured angrily as he surveyed the mess. 'All these fancy ideas about lynch mobs. A good boot in the belly would have got us all we needed.'

He turned to the mayor with a gesture of defeat while Jim Clark lit the lamp.

'I reckon you won't be wantin' to drink here. There's too much cleanin' up to do. Let's you and me go across to your place while young Jim puts things to rights.'

Mayor Bradley hastily agreed and the two men left the jailhouse for a more hospitable spot to talk and drink. The young deputy opened the cell and looked at the bodies. They had both been shot at close range and the position in which they lay seemed to indicate that somebody had stood on something outside the window and they had climbed on to their bunks to see who it was.

Jim Clark had no doubt that they had been killed to stop them talking, but what puzzled him was why no horses were heard galloping off. He wondered if the killer was still hiding in town. Or maybe lived in town.

FOUR

The cave went some thirty feet into the rock and its entrance was shielded by a copse of tall trees which swayed with the slightest breeze and rained clouds of fine dust. Somebody had built a frontage of horizontally laid logs on to the cave and there was a door and window. The place was a snug hideout which was difficult to spot against the reddish bareness of the hillside. A thin stream of clear water ran from a gully close by and there was enough grass to pasture a few horses or mules where they could not be seen from the trail.

It was the home of the Granton gang and Ma Granton had a hot meal ready for them when they returned from the bank raid on Bluff Point. She was a large woman who had once been quite attractive. Years of fierce suns and hard work looking after several men had coarsened her, but her brilliantly blue eyes were still sharp and dominating.

They took their horses round behind an outcrop of rock, unharnessed them and led them to the creek for a drink before looking to their own needs. When they entered the cabin, if it could be called that, Ma Granton's eyebrows rose on her seeing that three of the men were missing.

'What happened?' she asked tersely.

Alf Granton threw the bag of money on to the table and shook his head sadly.

'Matt's all right,' he said. 'He's tendin' his horse out at the creek. It's limpin' a bit and he's bathin' its fetlock. Cousin Ed and Wes Brooker got themselves caught. They was on the ground when we got the hell outa that damned awful town. It was hardly worth the trouble.'

Ma Granton picked up the bag and weighed it in her hand.

'How much?' she asked.

'Ain't had a chance to figure it out yet, but it sure ain't buyin' us a mansion in the East.'

He tipped the money out on the table while the others stood around to watch him count it.

'One hundred and twenty dollars, give or take a few cents,' Alf said despairingly. 'Wasn't hardly worth the journey. That damned manager had locked the safe and gone off with the townsfolk to unblock the creek.'

'We got a few watches, Pa,' Phil said as he put his share of the loot on the table. They all started to examine the gold and silver pocket-watches, all with chains attached and one with a tiny ruby pendant set in a gold frame. There were four silver vesta-cases and a small diamond stickpin.

'Maybe another hundred dollars or so,' Alf said grudgingly. 'What about the guns?'

Young Tom had the pistols in a sack that had originally been intended to carry the wealth of the Bluff Point bank. He pulled them out and laid them among the other trophies on the table. There were two .44 Colts, a .41 double-action Lightning, a .45 Colt that had seen better days, and a rather strange foreign gun that neither Ma Granton nor the two lads could identify.

Young Tom picked it up to examine it closely while his mother brought up another topic.

'Matt will be feelin' pretty bad if Ed's got hisself killed,' she said in a tone that was almost a warning.

Her husband glanced at her in a way that showed he understood her words.

'Ed Granton and Wes Brooker ain't necessarily dead,' he said quietly, 'but there's not much we can do about it anyways. If a fella takes up robbin' banks for a living, he's gotta face the risks that go with it.'

Ma Granton nodded. 'But Matt's a man who don't do much in the way of reasonin' things out,' she mused. 'He's got one hell of a short fuse.'

Alf glanced at his sons. 'There are three of us,' he said, 'and we at least have a few dollars to share out.' He turned to young Tom. 'Who was wearin' this gun, lad?' he asked sharply.

The young man blinked. He was not a fast thinker and stared at the weapon in his hand as though he had never seen it before. Then he shrugged his shoulders.

'I don't rightly know, Pa,' he murmured. 'There was five or six fellas in the bank and I just took every gun in sight.'

'Was it one of the clerks?'

'Could have been, and there was a fat fella with that derringer in his pocket. But I just don't recall.'

'Does it matter, Alf?' Ma Granton asked sharply. 'I want to set this table and put out the supper.'

Alf Granton took the strange gun from Tom and motioned the lads to clear the rest of the stuff away. He hung on to the gun and stroked it as though trying to prise some sort of story out of the thing. He examined the lacquered butt and toyed with the lanyard-ring. His gnarled fingers pushed up the chamber-cover as he extracted one of the cartridges and weighed it in his hand.

He went over to where Tom was helping his mother remove a roasted bird from the oven to the top of the stove.

'You gotta think about this gun, lad,' he said earnestly. 'You gotta picture yourself back in that

41

bank and try and recall who was carryin' this piece.'

The lad put the hot roasting-tin on the table and looked uneasily at his father.

'I'll try, Pa,' he promised, 'but everythin' was happenin' so quick.'

'Was the fella carryin' it in a holster?'

Tom stood silently for a moment.

'I don't rightly recall,' he admitted, 'but I reckon so.'

'What the hell is you on about, Alf Granton?'

It was his wife who snapped the words as she slapped heavy pewter plates on the table. 'You've yapped about that gun as though your life depended on it. We've just lost cousin Ed and Wes Brooker. Ain't that more important?'

The door opened before he could answer and cousin Matt entered. He was a short man, squarely built and with a wide, dark face and snub nose.

'I'd sure as hell say it was,' he snarled as he took off his hat and threw it in a corner. 'They could still be alive back there and bein' got ready for a hangin' right now.'

'There ain't nothin' we can do about that,' Phil Granton said before his father could reply.

'We could go back to that one-horse town and get them outa the jailhouse,' Matt shouted.

'Lookit, this is no time for fightin' among ourselves,' Alf said in a calming voice. 'It's taken us

42

the best part of two days to reach here, and it'd take us the same to get back to Bluff Point. Now, if they're still alive and the folks intended to hang them, they're long since dead. Lynch mobs don't wait around. And if they was goin' to be tried by the local judge, he'd have had time to do it by now and they'd be on their way to the territory jail. Either way, there ain't nothin' we can do.'

'We could try!' Matt shouted angrily.

Alf looked uncertain for a moment and then his eyes focussed on the gun in his hand.

'Maybe we could at that,' he aid softly. 'Maybe we could. Now, let's sit down to eat, and I'll tell you a tale you ain't heard before.'

Ma Granton put out the meal and the family tucked into the hot food. Cousin Matt was the only one who did not seem hungry but the others chewed away and looked at the jug of corn mash with greedy eyes. Alf Granton poured them all drinks and leaned forward to tell his tale.

'It was about twenty years ago,' he said slowly, 'and I was ridin' in them days with Uncle Billy and Huey Edwards. Uncle Billy had a fella who knew about the lumber camp up near Pellew Peak. This fellow had something to do with the bankin' business and told Uncle Billy that the wages were collected from Bluff Point every month. Knew all the details he did. So we set up a trap at the far end of a gorge about ten miles north of the town. Just laid a few rocks across the trail, we did. But it was enough to stop their wagon.'

He poured himself another drink and his wife held out her mug for a refill.

'It was like shootin' fish in a barrel,' Alf said in fond memory. 'There were four of them and we got one right away. Killed him stone-dead. The other three held out and we had a real shootin'-match for half an hour or more. Then it all went quiet. We climbed down from the rocks and found two more by the wagon. One was dead and the other wounded. Uncle Billy finished him off and we looked into the wagon for the payroll. But it weren't there, lads. We'd wasted our time.'

He wiped his mouth and looked round the table.

'What's the point of all this?' Matt asked impatiently.

'The point, lad, is that the fourth fella had gone off with the money. We rode after him but he'd had too good a start. We knew that he didn't have a horse, but there was just no way we could find him in all that tangle of scrub. All we got outa that deal was a mess of coffee, sugar, molasses, lamp-oil, and a few guns and saddles.'

'Sounds like the story of your life,' Ma Granton said drily.

Her husband ignored her.

'We figured that the fella had taken the payroll

on to the lumber camp. But when the hold-up was reported in the journals, it seemed he never showed up there. He'd made off with our money.'

'You do come across dishonest folk like that now and then.' Ma Granton laughed.

Nobody joined in her merriment. They were now too interested in Alf's story.

'So what's all this to us now?' Matt asked in a puzzled but interested voice.

'Well, we collected all the guns,' said Alf as he reached out to pick up the pistol that had intrigued him since first clapping eyes on it, 'but the fella who escaped with the money took his piece with him. And I reckon as how this is the one.'

He raised it in triumph and looked around the table as though expecting applause. They were all silent.

'Don't you realize what that means?' he shouted at them. 'Somebody in that bank was carryin' a gun that was worn by a fella who ran off with the lumber-camp payroll.'

There was a long silence as they chewed over what he had said. It was Phil, the brightest of the family, who eventually decided to speak.

'I ain't never seen a gun like that before, Pa,' he said thoughtfully, 'but there must be a hell of a lot more than one of them about. And it was all a long time ago. How can you be so certain?'

'The cartridge-cases, lad. When we was goin' through the goods on the wagon and takin' what we could carry, I noticed some empty cases on the ground. They was from a French gun called a Lefaucheaux. Just like these.'

He opened up the chamber cover again and used the lever to push out the remaining cartridges. They clattered on to the table and one ended up among the remains of Alf's meal.

'Look at 'em,' he said as he picked one up for their inspection. 'They're pin-fire. Somethin' that don't get used no more since Colt took over the market with centre-fire ammunition. In my young days, anyone who could afford one of these guns would sure as hell have one. They were replacin' the old Army and Navy Colts. Them damned Yankees bought thousands of them for their blue-bellies. They sold 'em off cheap after the war ended.'

'So there must be one hell of a lot of 'em around,' Phil said with blunt reason.

'No, son. There ain't. And 'cos why not? Colt and the Smith and Wesson fellas used cartridges that wouldn't damage so easy. The only man who'd have one of these things today would be some fella who didn't really need it. He'd have a sorta senti-mental feelin' for the thing, so he hangs on to it. And that fella lives in Bluff Point. He's a respectable citizen. Uses a bank and wears fancy clothes. Pillar of local society. Think about it. A fella like that has got one helluva lot to lose.'

Phil picked up one of the cartridges with its little pin sticking out of the side. He examined it closely and then tried to insert it back into the gun. It was a trickier job than loading his own Colt.

'You're tellin' us that he'd pay good money, Pa?' he suggested quietly.

'That's it, lad. He might be a storekeeper, or a lawyer. Could even be the mayor of that flea-bitten place. He sure as hell won't be wantin' folks to know that he once made off with his boss's payroll. That he's a no-good thievin' sorta fella, just like us.'

Ma Granton poured herself some more corn liquor.

'So how come he went to settle in Bluff Point?' she asked. 'Folk might have recognized him, and the timber fellas would be goin' into town from time to time. It'd be one hell of a dangerous place to live.'

Alf looked uncertain for a moment.

'Well, let's work it out,' he aid slowly. 'This fella makes off with the money, but he's on foot. He can't travel very far, and Bluff Point is the only town within spittin' distance. He'd lie low for a while, maybe gettin' work on ranches. Then he goes into town when he's all nicely shaved, duded up, and lookin' a very different sorta fella from what he was a few months earlier. He could stake himself to a good business, settle down, and be all respectable. I reckon that's what he'd do. But he kept his gun, and we got it now.'

'So where does this help us with Ed and Wes?' Matt asked bluntly.

'One of us goes into town and makes a few enquiries. Folks are gonna be in a talkative mood after what happened back there. There's a gun store in Bluff Point, and the fella that runs it can help us one hell of a lot.'

'And who goes into town?' Phil asked.

Alf Granton was silent for a moment, and then he threw a nervous glance at his wife.

'I figure as how Ma should be the one to go,' he said in a small voice.

'Are you outa your applejack-soaked mind, Alf Granton?' she shrieked at him. 'That's one hell of a journey in a two-wheeled buggy like that old bone-shaker we got. And how the hell can I go into a store and start askin' questions about fancy guns with names I can't even say?'

'Now, calm it, Ma,' Alf pleaded. 'I got that figured out. Somethin' might give us away if any of us go. Even if we shaved and looked innocent as farm boys off to sing in the choir, there might be something that would be noticed by some smart-eyed fella. But you'd be just a woman goin' to town for supplies. And I've already figured out how you can ask about the gun. So don't fret.'

'I should go,' Matt said in a sour, demanding voice. 'It's my brother back there.'

'No, Matt,' Alf assured him. 'You're too valuable for other things. Ma can find out about Ed and Wes just as well as you can. And she won't be noticed none. I need you to ride out to Chris Machin and sell them guns and watches. You always do a better trade than I do. He's scared to hell because you ain't got my friendly disposition.'

Matt thought it over for a moment and fell for the flattery as was intended. He nodded his head contentedly and held out his glass for Ma to refill it.

'You ain't sellin' this fancy French gun to old Machin, are you, Pa?' Phil asked.

Alf grinned. 'Hell, no, son. This is gonna keep us in food and drink for a long, long time.'

FIVE

The woman who drove the two-wheeled rig was large and plainly dressed. Her greying hair was pulled back in a bun and her brilliantly blue eyes scanned the street with casual ease. Nobody paid much attention to her as she stopped outside the grocery store and got down to hitch the elderly mare to the rail. She put on its feed bag and looked around.

Bluff Point's main street was quite busy. It was near to noon, the women were shopping and the children were due to be released from the slavery of the schoolroom. Marshal Welsby dozed on the stoop of the jailhouse and the Lady Luck saloon was getting its first customers of the day.

Ma Granton took a canvas shopping-bag from the buggy and hitched up her skirt a little to mount the single wooden step to the food store. As she did so, something appeared to catch her attention and she bent to pick it up. The sunlight

50

glinted on a small brass item that she held close to her eyes and turned around with noticeable curiosity. Then she shrugged, shoved it into the pocket of her skirt, and entered the store.

There were a couple of other women there and she was able to look around for a few moments. When it was her turn to be served, she took out her list, reeled off the items, and added a few things to suit her own tastes. Sunnyside coffee was one of her favourites, and she bought some of Our Mother's Cocoa as a special evening treat. While the goods were being packed into her bag by an attentive storekeeper, she felt in her pocket for the money, and also took out the little piece of brass.

'What do you make of that?' she asked casually. 'I just picked it up on the stoop.'

The storekeeper took it off her and turned it over in his fingers. He smiled as though remembering things of times past.

'Ain't seen one of these in a coon's age,' he said as he handed it back. 'It's a cartridge-case for one of them foreign guns that was so popular in my young days. Them Yankees got rid of a lot of 'em cheap after the war and my pa sold ten of the things to local folks. Sure got old Charlie Payne mad as a hornet. He was runnin' the gun store at the time and hadn't the sense to make the deal with the drummer.'

'Then there must be quite a few of them

around,' Ma Granton suggested.

'Bless you, no, ma'am. The Colts took over and there's nary a one in town these days, except for . . .'

His eyes suddenly dulled and he started arranging the groceries in the bag for a second time.

'Just ain't no call for 'em, ma'am,' he said flatly as he escorted his customer to the door and placed the groceries in the buggy. Mrs Granton thanked him and walked down the street to look in the linen store. There were things there she fancied, but Ma Granton was a careful woman and likely to make do with what she had unless it was past mending. She visited the hardware store and chatted to a few other women before coming out into the sunlight again.

Her next call was to Wally Payne's gun store. Charlie was long since dead, but his lanky, large-nosed son was running it with the aid of an apprentice. The window was a small one with only a couple of shotguns and a Winchester on display. There were a few tinted posters advertising ammunition and a collection of gunbelts and holsters.

Ma Granton entered the place and found herself the only customer. Wally was at the counter, cleaning a second-hand shotgun which he put down at the rare sight of a woman in his store.

'And what can I do for you on this fine day,

ma'am?' he asked with a slightly sarcastic polite-
ness.

'I want some ammunition,' Ma Granton said
firmly.

She scanned the glass-topped counter with a
practised eye and tapped on the glass above a
brown carton that bore a green Winchester label.

'Is that a box of twenty?' she asked.

'Yes, ma'am, forty-calibre Sharps rifle.'

'Give me two boxes.'

She moved along the counter, scanning the
ammunition until her eyes lighted on another
carton. She tapped again on the glass with a
small metallic thing that she held between her
fingers.

'And a box of .45,' she said.

Wally Payne removed the cartons dutifully and
placed them before her on the counter. She
looked at the little cartridge-case in her hand as
though seeing it for the first time.

'What is this funny little thing?' she asked in an
innocent voice. 'I just picked it up in the street.'

'That, ma'am, is a .41 Lefaucheaux cartridge-
case. Pin-fire.'

'Ain't never seen nothin' like it in all my life. I
thought it might be somethin' useful.'

'No, ma'am. Just scrap metal these days. That
little pin thing would break off too easy, so it faded
away like sling-shots and bows an' arrows.'

'Do you still get a call for them?' Ma asked.

'No, ma'am. They're as dead as Abe Lincoln.'

He took Ma Granton's money and watched her leave. He had started work on the shotgun again before a thought struck him. Wally Payne cursed under his breath as he took a small carton of pin-fire ammunition out of the glass case and hid it behind some other boxes on a shelf.

Ma Granton left town without noticing the man who watched her from the Lady Luck saloon. Matt Granton had left his horse out of sight, had shaved neatly, and looked a very different man as he nursed his whiskey at the window of the saloon.

He had done a deal with old Machin. The guns and watches were sold at a good price, but now he wanted to find out what had happened to his brother and Wes Brooker. He did not risk going near the jailhouse or the bank, but felt it was safe to take a quiet drink and wait for folks to come in and start talking.

It should be easy to find out about the recent hold-up. It would still be the main topic of interest in such a small place. He waited impatiently until some drunk would put in an appearance and shoot off his mouth for a few free drinks. He could see the marshal on the jailhouse stoop, but there was no sign of the deputy.

The deputy was not far away. Young Jim Clark was a puzzled man. He had checked the rear of the jailhouse after the killings and found no signs of horses having been near it. A small barrel had been upturned and moved from its usual place beneath a drainpipe. It was now under the high window and somebody had stood on it to shoot the two occupants of the cell. The marshal had agreed with him on that point, but was not interested in who might have done it.

But Jim Clark was interested. He had thought at first that the men were killed because they could identify their companions in the hold-up and lead the marshal to their hideout. But the other three raiders had fled the town and were not likely to have risked coming back again so soon. He kept his own counsel and also kept a watchful eye on whatever was happening in Bluff Point.

Jim had already spotted Matt Granton drinking in the Lady Luck saloon, and had checked on his horse at the livery-stable corral. It told him nothing, and the man looked like a ranch hand or a small farmer. He carried a gun at his waist but no shotgun or rifle, and was clean and well dressed. The deputy could not recall having seen him around town before, but he seemed a peaceful sort of fellow and was not drinking too much or bothering anyone.

Jim Clark had also noticed Ma Granton but had

paid no attention to her shopping trip. It surprised him that she went into the gun store, but a woman did occasionally buy ammunition for her husband while in town to do other chores. Then he saw something that really did puzzle him. Wally Payne came out of the gun store and crossed the street to the jailhouse. He woke the marshal and the two stood talking for a while.

After a bit the marshal crossed the street with Wally, and while the gunsmith went into his own building, Ethan Welsby walked a little further along to enter the food store. He came out after a few minutes and stood on the stoop. He stroked his chin thoughtfully and had a slightly worried look on his face. Jim Clark drew back into the shadow of the schoolhouse so that he would not be seen.

He watched his boss for a few more minutes as the marshal hovered uncertainly between going back to snooze on the jailhouse stoop, or doing something more positive. Jim decided to approach him and see what was going on. He walked casually up the main street until the lawman spotted him. Ethan waved wildly and Jim Clark hurried to join him.

'Been lookin' for you, lad,' the marshal said urgently. 'A woman's just left town drivin' a two-wheeled rig. I want you to get after her and see where she's heading.'

'Do we know who she is, Marshal?' Jim asked.

'No, she's a stranger, but I wanta find out where she's from. Could be one of them squatters up along the creek, or maybe she's from some small-holdin' down Hayford way. Just get on her tail and don't lose her.'

'Suppose she's travellin' overnight?'

'Take a bite of food with you,' the lawman said impatiently. 'A lone woman won't travel far, so move your ass before you lose her trail.'

Jim Clark asked no more questions and did as he was told. The marshal felt contented enough to go across to the Lady Luck for a drink. He moved in his stately fashion and mounted the step of the well-appointed saloon. There were only a few customers and he knew all but one of them. The bartender automatically placed the whiskey in front of him and the lawman raised the glass thankfully to his lips.

His eyes rested on the stranger who had moved from the window and now stood near him at the bar. The stranger was a neat-looking fellow who could have been a ranch hand.

'Passin' through?' the marshal asked as he made sure that his badge was well displayed.

The man nodded.

'Cattle-buyin' up Lingfield way,' he said in a friendly voice. 'My horse needed a rest and I'm feelin' a bit thirsty myself. Nice town you have here, Marshal. Peaceful sort of place, I should imagine.'

The lawman drew himself up.

'We have our moments,' he said in a modest voice. 'The bank was held up a few days ago. Quite a shoot-out there was.'

'Is that a fact now? Did you get 'em?'

'I sure as blazes did. A few got away but I shot the hell outa two of them, and the ones that escaped had less than five hundred dollars. Must have been the least successful bank raid for many a year.'

The set of the stranger's mouth grew tight and his words came with difficulty through gritted teeth.

'Less than five hundred dollars,' he mused. 'Was that all the money your bank had?'

'Hell, no, but the bankin' fella had the safe locked and the key hid in the waste basket. All they picked up was what was behind the counter and three hundred dollars he had on his desk. They was surely the biggest bunch of rubes you ever did see.'

He then remembered his brave and totally invented role.

'They was tough though. Shootin' mad in all directions, they was. Nearly got me and my deputy, but I've been a lawman a long time and I know my job.'

Matt Granton stepped back a couple of feet and put down his glass.

'You sure do, Marshal,' he said quietly. 'But I'm here to tell you that one of them fellas you shot was my brother. And I don't take kindly to that. You've got a gun, so draw.'

Marshal Welsby's mouth gaped open and his mind did not seem to work as he stared at the angry face of the man in front of him. The few drinkers in the saloon were not in earshot of the words the two had spoken. The lawman had not wanted them to hear his idle boasting, and Matt Granton was too furious to shout. It was all he could do to get the words out as he confronted the man he thought had killed his brother.

His hand went down to the Colt at his belt and he drew it smoothly, with his thumb pulling back the hammer. One of the other drinkers realized what was happening and nudged the man at his side. They both headed for the door, still holding their glasses in their panic to be out of range.

The marshal's whiskey fell from his fist as he fumbled for his own gun. His shaking fingers reached the butt as a shot echoed round the room and he staggered back. Ethan Welsby's face crumpled with pain as his shattered left arm hit the counter and scattered the glasses that lay there. They rolled noisily around while he struggled to pull his gun and shoot back.

It came out of the holster, his thumb feeling for the hammer as the second shot hit him. It was more accurate this time and the bullet entered his chest. Ethan Welsby slid to the sawdusted floor and hardly moved again.

SIX

Ma Granton was weary and covered in trail dust when she got back to the cave that the family called their home. Alf and the two lads came out to greet her, unhitching the horse and taking in her baggage. Alf poured a cup of coffee and she swallowed it thankfully as she sat at the table.

'How did it go, Ma?' he asked anxiously.

'It's one hell of a journey to that one-horse town,' she moaned. 'I near caught a chill out there on the range, and I still feel I'm a nestin' place for every spider and roach in the territory. But you were right, Alf. That bullet case is somethin' to think about.'

Her two sons came in while she was telling her husband about the reactions of both store-owners when they saw the pin-fire case in her hand.

'They sure as hell had somethin' to hide,' she said, 'and that fella in the gun store had a pack of them cartridges in the glass case. It looked like it

61

had been there for quite a while, but he was certainly keepin' them bullets in stock.'

'So that gun does belong to one of the town dudes,' Alf mused, 'and other folks is protectin' him. He must be important.'

'I reckon so,' his wife agreed. 'I also heard tell about Ed and Wes. They was shot in the jailhouse.'

'In the jailhouse?' Alf's voice rose in pitch.

'That's what folks say. I spoke to a coupla women back there, and they told me that some fella shot them both through the cell window. Never did find out who done it, and I reckon they don't care none.'

'Well, ain't that a hell of a thing to happen? Somebody must have been real mad at us for robbin' that bank.'

Ma Granton looked around. 'Matt not back yet?' she asked.

'No, but I figure on him spendin' some of the money on whiskey before he turns up here. We can't grudge him a few drinks and he always does a good deal with old Machin.'

'Ain't that the truth. He scares the hell outa the old critter.'

They all laughed and began unpacking the goods that had been bought in Bluff Point. Then it was time for a meal and a quiet sit-down in front of the stove with hot coffee and corn mash.

*

The lamp was lit and Alf Granton was dozing in his rocking-chair when the door opened noisily and Matt came in with his saddlebags across his left arm. He dumped them on the floor and looked round the warm room. Ma Granton got up to pour him some coffee while Alf picked up the whiskey flagon that sat by his chair. The two younger men grinned their welcome and then went back to playing cards.

'Made a good deal?' Alf asked eagerly as he poured corn mash into an enamel mug for the newcomer.

Matt took the mug and drank deep. A thin film of dust fell from his clothes as he banged the empty container down on the table.

'Good enough,' he growled, wiping his mouth. 'One hundred and twenty-two dollars. And the old man sent his thanks for the trade.'

'Does he still smell like an angry skunk?' Ma asked, adding sugar to the coffee.

'Just about. How did you get on in Bluff Point, Ma?'

He listened carefully as she related her experiences there. There was a little hesitation before she told him what had happened to his brother and Wes Brooker. Matt's face drained of colour when he heard how they had been killed.

'Well, that sure as hell beats everything,' he muttered angrily.

'Better than bein' hanged, I reckon,' Alf said unfeelingly.

'But who shot 'em, Pa?' young Tom asked quietly. 'They was only bank robbers and they didn't hurt nobody. The judge wouldn't have hanged them and there weren't much money involved. So why kill 'em?'

They all looked at him for a moment and then at Phil who was regarded as the brightest of the family. He just shrugged his shoulders and started to deal another hand of cards. It was Matt who made the next move. He took the money from his pocket and laid it on the table.

'Let's work out the split,' he said. 'I aim to make tracks in the morning.'

'What the hell for?' Alf asked angrily. 'There's plenty of other banks and we got a few dollars to tide us over.'

'I went to Bluff Point,' Matt said in a neutral voice. 'That's why I took so long gettin' back. Ed and me was family and I had to know what happened to him. That damned marshal boasted that he killed both of 'em when they was gettin' out of town. Well, we knew that they was brought down off their horses, so I believed him.'

'And you had a shoot-out.' Ma shook her head grimly. 'You always was a hot-headed fella, Matt Granton.'

'Yeah. It was a fool thing to do, maybe, but Ed

was my kid brother. If I stick around with you, the law's gonna paint you all with the same tar brush as me. You could all be in for a hangin' if we get caught together.'

Alf nodded sadly.

'That makes sense,' he murmured, 'and I'm beholden to you for thinkin' that way, Matt. We'll make the share-out now, and I reckon nobody will mind you takin' all of Ed's cut.'

He looked around the family and all heads nodded their silent agreement.

'Well, I thank you for that,' Matt said quietly. He watched Alf open the bag of bank money and tip it out next to the contribution from the sale of the guns and other items.

'You'd better do the dividin' of it, Phil,' Alf said with a grin, 'seein' as how you're the one with all the learnin' from the Blue Back spellin'-book.'

'I saw that he got some learning,' Ma Granton said proudly.

'There's three hundred dollars short,' Matt said in a low, taut voice.

The others looked at him in amazement.

'What the hell do you mean by that?' Alf asked in bewilderment. 'You know full well this is all we got from the bank.'

'You went into the manager's office,' Matt said, 'and he had three hundred dollars laid out on his desk. He locked the safe and hid the key. Said he was only a clerk and fooled you outa the rest of the money. But you got that three hundred dollars and I want my share.'

Alf Granton looked to his two sons for support but realized that nobody could back his story. He had been alone in the manager's office.

'Lookit, Matt,' he protested hoarsely, 'we're family and I wouldn't pull a no-good trick like that. All we got was what you fellas collected from the clerks. There was no money on the desk and the little fella there was just some old clerk lookin' after things while the boss was outa town.'

Matt shook his head stubbornly.

'That ain't so,' he insisted. 'The marshal weren't the only fella to tell me that tale. Other folk in Bluff Point knew that another three hundred dollars was took by us. So lay it on the table, Alf, before I gets real mean about it.'

The threat was clear and Matt Granton still carried a gun at his waist. None of the other men was armed. Their guns lay on shelves or on hooks around the warm room.

'Matt, I am tellin' the God's honest truth,' Alf protested. 'I ain't stole a red cent of the cash. It's all here. That marshal—'

'I ain't relyin' on a loud-mouthed boaster like him,' Matt said as he backed from the table and let his right hand slide down towards the holster.

'Others was tellin' the same tale.'

He turned to Ma Granton who stood like a rock with the coffee-pot in her hand.

'You were in town, Ginny,' he said. 'What did you pick up about the bank job?'

She looked at her husband and sons.

'I didn't hear nothin' about no three hundred dollars,' she said loyally.

'You're all in on it,' Matt insisted savagely.

He reached down for the Colt and it seemed to fly into his hand with the loud click of the hammer echoing around the room. Alf jumped backwards in alarm and bumped into the table. His sons leapt from their seats to dodge the shot, but it never came.

Ma Granton flung the coffee-pot and it struck the angry man in the neck as he raised the weapon to shoot his cousin. He let out a yell as the scalding coffee sprayed all over him while the Colt dropped from his hand.

It was Phil who picked it up from the floor. He took careful aim and shot the writhing man in the chest. The noise was deafening in the small space and then a silence fell as Matt Granton slipped to the ground. He twitched for a few minutes while they watched him in silence. Then he rolled over on his side and lay still.

Ma Granton picked up the coffee-pot and placed it at the side of the stove. She looked hard at her shaken husband as he tried to recover his poise as head of the household.

'I heard the same tale Matt heard,' she said coldly. 'Folks was talkin' about it all over town.'

SEVEN

Young Jim Clark lay behind a clump of bushes and watched the screen of tall trees that covered the reddish outline of the slope. He could not see the cave with its wooden frontage but he could occasionally hear the sounds of horses grazing somewhere close by.

He had had no trouble following Ma Granton for the best part of two days as she journeyed home. She had taken things easily, stopping for the night by a small creek and nursing her horse over the rough trail. It was dark now and he had seen her go through the screen of trees and heard the sound of voices greeting her. There were glimpses of lamplight and the smell of cooking food as the branches moved in the wind.

Jim also saw the second arrival. Matt Granton rode a large bay horse and guided it through the trees with ease in the steady moonlight.

Then there was a shot. It was loud in the darkness and scared a few nesting birds. Jim listened carefully but all fell silent again as he patiently watched.

He had already determined to return to town the next morning. He had the information the marshal needed, and he had a little extra. The young deputy had seen Matt Granton enter the Lady Luck saloon, and he thought it strange that neither he nor the woman should acknowledge each other in town, yet both end up in the same place.

The young lawman did not know why Marshal Welsby was so anxious to locate the woman. He had seen his boss talking to the two store-owners, and she had entered both places. He wondered if she had stolen something or tried some flim-flam trick. But even that made little sense. She could have been arrested in town. Unless she was part of a gang and the rest of them were there behind the trees.

Jim Clark looked up at the scudding clouds and the position of the moon. He waited until it was hidden enough for him to bend low and move towards the row of sycamores that sheltered the cave. The wind was strong and gusty. It dropped fine sprays of dust on him as the branches swayed and the cold pierced his thin shirt and leather waistcoat. He could catch glimpses of lamplight in the window of the log-built frontage, and there was a faint sound of voices.

The door suddenly opened and light flooded out. He hugged the grassy earth as the voices became louder and figures appeared outlined by the lamps or candles behind them. He raised his head to get a look at what was going on. Two men were carrying a body from the cabin.

He watched as they dumped it a few yards from the building, and then went back inside and closed the door. He could still hear voices, which seemed to be raised in anger. A woman appeared to dominate and the young deputy crawled forward to see who had been killed by the shot he had heard.

As he reached the body, the moon came out from behind its thin veil of cloud to give him a better view. It was the man he had seen in town, who had arrived after the woman. He had been shot in the chest.

Jim moved slowly back to the line of trees, recovered his horse, and went off to get some sleep for what was left of the night. He set out for Bluff Point at dawn.

Ma Granton was the first one awake in the morning. She and her husband had a small room to themselves at the back of the structure, and he was still snoring when she went out to the main room. She ignored her two sleeping sons, and began lighting the stove. She opened the door to let in some fresh air and breathed deeply as the breeze ruffled her greying locks. She took the wooden pail as usual round to the outcrop of the rocky hill where the clear water of the stream ran from somewhere high above the tree-line. The horses watched her as she passed Matt's body without a glance.

He would be buried later when the lads had finished their breakfast. Ma Granton was still angry about what had happened the night before, and was still not sure that her husband's innocent. Alf was not the most honest of men and they had had a blazing row after removing Matt's body from the cabin. Phil and Tom contributed little to it. They were in awe of their father. But Ma Granton was not. She was in awe of nobody.

She washed her face in the cool water, filled the bucket, and trudged back towards the cabin. When she reached Matt's corpse, she stopped to look at it. There was no sentiment in her inspection. It was simply the need to see if there was anything of value that should be removed before he was put under the ground.

Her sharp eyes noticed something that should not have been there and she stood silently for several moments, looking hard at the earth around the body.

There were the footmarks of her two sons, etched sharply in the gravel, but there were extra prints that came from the line of sycamores, and went back there. Some other person had been outside the cabin last night.

Ma Granton hurried back to wake the two lads. She also gave Alf a dig in the ribs, and gathered them all in the main room. She then explained what she had seen and waited impatiently while they ran out to prove her words by personal inspections.

'You was followed from town, Ma,' Tom said reproachfully.

Phil shook his head.

'No, I don't reckon that to be the case. It was Matt who was followed. He killed that marshal and headed straight for this place. Somebody trailed him sure as shooting.'

Alf agreed. 'Must only be one fella,' he mused, 'or they'd have taken us durin' the night. Let's shovel Matt under ground and then get the blazes outa here for some place safer.'

'Where in hell can we go?' Ma Granton asked despairingly.

'Any place would be better than here if a posse turns up,' Alf snapped. 'There's a miner's cabin up by Womanda Creek. It's not much but it's off the trail and there's a little water most of the year.'

Ma nodded agreement. 'Get Matt under ground, lads,' she ordered. 'I'll cook some food, and then we'll pack and get the hell out.'

The stove was hot enough now to fry the bacon, and she began to prepare a meal. Her husband stood at her side, watching the busy hands moving above the skillet.

'I never did take that money, Ma,' he said quietly. 'I mighta held out on Matt and the others, but not on you and the boys. You know me better than that.'

She gave him a quick glance and there was a hint of a smile on her face.

'I know that,' she said, 'but I was sure angry at the time. You understand what this means, don't you, Alf?'

He looked blank and Ma Granton turned the bacon over before answering his unspoken question.

'That bank manager pocketed the extra three hundred dollars,' she said. 'He took his own bank for it, and blamed you.'

Her husband's face cracked into a wide grin.

'Well, ain't that the top prize in the turkey-shoot!' he exclaimed. 'We got a fella who made off with a payroll, and a crooked bank manager, both livin' in the same town. Nice respectable dudes who'll pay right well to keep their little secrets. If that don't beat holdin' up banks, I don't know what does.'

'It could be dangerous, Alf,' Ma Granton warned him. 'One of us has to go into town, and them two fellas will be real desperate to save their hides.'

'Yeah.' He nodded. 'We gotta work it all out careful-like. Did the folks you talked to in Bluff Point have any idea who killed Ed and Wes?'

'No names were mentioned but I reckon I know.'

'And we can make a few dollars on it?' Alf asked eagerly.

'I guess so, if we don't get killed a'doin' it.'

Her husband scratched the side of his face as he thought over the solution.

'We could use old Uncle Billy,' he suggested quietly. 'He was leadin' the gang when we raided that payroll wagon, and he had some bank fella feedin' him information.'

His wife looked doubtful.

'Your Uncle Billy is a liar, a cheat, a thief, a flim-flam man, and as treacherous as any politician you could spit on.'

Alf grinned. 'Just the fella for the job,' he agreed.

EIGHT

Jim Clark rode slowly back home. He was tired, hungry, and puzzled by the whole thing. It was past noon when he reached Bluff Point. The day was hot but cloudy, and the main street was quiet as folks took their meals. He found the door of the jailhouse locked and the young deputy stood undecided for a moment, looking up and down the street for any sign of Marshal Welsby.

He glanced across at the hardware store and could see the mayor through the window. He wore his white apron and was serving a customer with a large coil of the new-fangled barbed wire. They came out, carrying it carefully to load on a small wagonette. The mayor stood on the stoop and waved the man off.

Jim Clark crossed the street to see what Jess Bradley knew about the jailhouse being closed. The First Citizen had already seen him and was waiting with an expression of annoyance on his scrawny face.

'You've been gone a helluva time, young fella,' he greeted the deputy.

'The marshal sent me—'

The mayor waved a dismissive hand.

'I know all about the woman you was following,' he snapped. 'Wally Payne told me what happened. But why was you so long? You was needed here.'

'Where's the marshal?' Jim Clark asked.

The mayor looked at him in surprise before realizing that the deputy knew nothing of events in town. He told the young man of the shooting, and of how Ethan Welsby had been chief guest at the biggest funeral of the year.

'But how did he get the drop on the marshal?' Jim asked. 'And why did he kill him?'

Mayor Bradley took the young man by the arm and led him into the store. Mrs Bradley was behind the long counter and Jim tipped his hat to her as he was led into the back room which Jess Bradley used as the mayoral office. The two sat down at the desk, and for the first time, Jim Clark was treated to a share of the best whiskey.

'We don't know why it happened,' he was told. 'Ethan was talkin' peaceable-like to this stranger, and all of a sudden, there's gunplay. The fella told him to draw, and Ethan was a bit too slow. Got shot clean in the chest and that was that. Then this fella goes off before anybody can get their wits about them. It's surely a mystery.'

'What was this stranger like?' Jim asked. He was beginning to work out the possibilities.

The mayor described Matt Granton with considerable accuracy. The deputy nodded as he grasped the sequence of events.

'I met up with him,' he said carefully, 'and he won't be drawin' on no more marshals.'

The mayor's eyes brightened and he put down his glass with a bang.

'You killed him?' he asked eagerly.

'He's as dead as Abe Lincoln,' he was told calmly, 'and that woman the marshal sent me to trail may be in cahoots with him. They was both headin' in the same direction.'

'The hell they was!' Mayor Bradley suddenly looked a little nervous. 'So where is she now?'

Jim told him, and taking a piece of paper from the desk, he drew a rough map of the area.

'There are three or four more fellas with her,' he explained, 'and I figure as how they're the ones who robbed the bank.'

'Does she know you was on her tail?'

'I reckon not. I was careful.'

The mayor sat thoughtfully for a while. His nervous fingers tapped the desk and the whiskey remained untouched.

'Why was I asked to follow the woman?' Jim asked.

The question dragged Jess Bradley out of his reverie.

'Oh, that,' he murmured. 'Well, there are some things that the older folks in town know that are kinda private-like. You can see how it is when families have lived in the same place for a lotta years. We sorta look after each other. It's only natural, Jim. Only natural. Wally Payne recalled seein' her from years back and told the marshal that she was a shady character.'

The mayor's words seemed to taper off and he took a quick swill of the whiskey to give him courage.

'Lookit, lad, you are gonna take over here as marshal, and that means that you will be gettin' your orders from the town council. Through me. There are things we'll tell you when the time comes, and we know you better. But for now, just do the work and don't get too nosy. Understand?'

'I guess so, Mr Mayor, and thanks for givin' me the job.'

'You're worth it, lad. And when folks hear that you've located the bank robbers and already killed the fella as shot our marshal, you'll be one hell of a hero.'

He poured out more whiskey and leaned across the desk.

'Now, here's your first big job, Marshal,' he said in his official voice. 'We'll get a posse together and we'll deal with them robbers. And we don't want them alive either. The council gets real sore at the cost of trials and the antics of lawyers. Just a good shootin'-match, and that's an end to it. Bury them where you find them. You understand me?'

Jim smiled. 'Sure do, Mr Mayor.'

'So get on with it, lad. Oh, and one more thing. Them fellas stole guns and watches from the folks in the bank that day. They'd sure appreciate havin' them back. See what you can do. It'll make you real popular.' He grinned. 'And me too. We always gotta think of elections.'

Jim stood up to go and then turned to confront the mayor.

'Who do you figure shot the two men in the jail-house?' he asked casually.

The question took Jess Bradley by surprise.

'Well, I can't say as I've given it much thought,' he admitted, 'but I always reckoned as how the other bank robbers did it to stop them talkin' about hideouts. I guess that makes sense.'

'That's what the marshal and me thought at first,' Jim said quietly, 'but they'd be on horseback, and there weren't no fresh signs of horses round the back of the jailhouse. And that don't make a lotta sense, Mr Mayor.'

Jess Bradley thought about it for a moment as he

put the cork back in the whiskey bottle.

'Are you suggestin' someone local?' he asked.

'Could be.'

'But why? In hell's name, why?'

'Maybe someone wanted to make sure they never came to trial and spoke out in court.'

'That would make sense, but what would they have said in court, Jim?'

The new marshal took a deep breath before answering.

'It could be that not as much money was stole as we was told,' he ventured.

There was a long silence while Jess Bradley put away the bottle and came back to the desk.

'That would be suggestin' that our good citizen, George Cullen, ain't as honest a man as we take him to be.'

There was a slight irony in the mayor's voice and his eyebrow was raised quizzically.

'Well, he was fast enough to close the safe and hide the key,' Jim said, 'and if he had the wits to do that, I'd have figured him for lockin' up that three hundred dollars and not leavin' it on the desk. Wouldn't you?'

The mayor grinned, and his thin face lit up with an unholy delight.

'Them words warm my old heart, lad,' he said happily. 'That palsied old go-to-meetin' money-lender has lorded it in this town for a coon's age.

Looks down his nose at workin' folks like us, and sings hymns louder than the preacher every blessed Sunday. So he's as big a thief as the fellas what took his bank.'

He looked sharply at the new marshal. 'But can we prove it?'

'I doubt it, Mr Mayor, and I could be wrong.'

'Oh, no. I don't think so, lad. I don't think so.'

The mayor seemed to hesitate for a moment and then invited Jim to sit down again.

'There used to be a lumber company used our bank when they was workin' up on the tree-line around the northern ridges,' Jess Bradley said slowly. 'They had to collect the payrolls every month, and it was done very quiet-like without folk knowin' any details. A wagon would make its usual pick-up of food and suchlike, and a few men from the lumber camp would ride in at the same time and leave with the wagon. The payroll would be hidden among the supplies.'

The mayor looked longingly at the cupboard where he had placed the whiskey.

'Then the payroll was stolen one day. They was bushwhacked by a gang and all but one of them killed. The bank investigators and them Pinkerton fellas the timber company hired, all reckon as how the hold-up men were tipped off. Either a clerk in the company or somebody in our bank. I was wonderin' if maybe George Cullen was the fella.

I'd like to think so, and it would explain a few things. Him and that scraggy wife of his have always lived high on the hog.'

'You said all but one, Mr Mayor.' Jim's voice was flat and devoid of interest.

'What? Oh, yeah, but that's another story. You have yourself some rest while I go round and see what we can do about a posse. I'll call a meetin' of the townsfolk and we'll deal with them raiders.'

The mayor did not have a lot of luck. He only mustered seven men after enough talking to have got him elected to the legislature. And then none of the posse would leave home until the next morning. There was not much enthusiasm for chasing after bandits who had taken so little money and who were two days' ride away.

Jim Clark led them out of Bluff Point just as the sun was breaking through a thin veil of cloud. He wore a marshal's badge now and had already gained respect as the man who shot Ethan Welsby's killer.

He had a worry of his own that nagged at him during the journey. He had never actually said that he shot Matt Granton, and he wondered what had happened to the body back at the cabin. If it still lay unburied, he was going to have some awkward questions to answer.

His anxiety reached its peak when the line of

trees was approached and he had to lead his rather timid collection of would-be heroes towards the hideout. They crouched in the undergrowth, peering at the wooden wall in front of the cave and looking for movement of some sort. Nothing happened, and to precipitate events, Jim ordered a volley of shots to be fired.

There was no reply and they moved forward across the open space with more confidence. The cabin lay deserted. The stove was cold and everything portable had gone. There were no animals around and no sign of Matt's body. Jim breathed a sigh of relief, and when he saw some disturbed earth near the corral, he was careful to steer the others away from it.

'Well, I guess we've seen the last of them fellas,' one of the posse said as if regretting the lack of a fight.

Jim looked at the men around him and nodded his head as though in agreement.

'Yeah, I reckon,' he muttered. 'Let's head for home.'

NINE

The man who rode into Bluff Point was a striking figure on a large black gelding. He was certainly in his sixties but carried himself well and had a grey moustache against a tanned, once handsome face. His trail-coat was covered in dust and the saddle-bags bulged with his belongings. He looked as if he had ridden a long way.

He stopped at the rear of the bank, dismounted with a slightly stiff posture and then stretched himself to ease the strain of a long time in the saddle. There was a water-trough near by and he led his horse to it. He then took off the trail-coat, laid it across the saddlebags and dusted off the large Stetson which topped his ample head of grey hair. His coat was that of a sober citizen of means, and even the gun at his side did not diminish the air of respectable command which he radiated.

He walked round the corner to the front of the building and looked around confidently. The

Stetson was raised to a passing female as he entered the bank and approached the counter. There was only one customer and the clerk looked up from his ledger, eager to deal with the newcomer.

'I wish to see the manager,' the stranger said in a loud, almost theatrical voice.

'You got an appointment?' the clerk asked.

The stranger took what appeared to be a large wad of banknotes from his pocket. The man behind the counter could see the top five-dollar bill. He gulped slightly and moved towards the office.

'I'll go tell Mr Cullen,' he said meekly.

He almost ran into the manager's room and emerged a moment or two later with George Cullen right behind. The banker had a welcoming smile on his thin face as the prospect of a rich new customer loomed before him.

'My dear sir,' he greeted the stranger as he thrust out a dry hand, 'please come into my office and take a slight refreshment.'

The stranger smiled as they shook hands. Both men had firm grips but the bank manager suddenly seemed as though he had been stricken by some strange paralysis. His eyes were staring at the man in front of him and he had paled as his hand was wrung with enthusiasm.

He followed the stranger into the office and

closed the door as though in a trance. The man sat down at the desk and waited while the stricken money-lender poured out a whiskey before sitting down himself.

'Your face . . . ?' George Cullen ventured hesitantly. 'It's very familiar. Should I know you?'

The visitor grinned to disclose perfect teeth.

'You know me, George,' he said, raising his glass. 'At least, you did twenty years ago. When you was a bank clerk in this one-eyed hole. Don't you remember Billy Granton?'

'Oh, my God!' The banker looked stricken. 'I thought you'd be dead long ago. Or in jail.'

'Neither, and I don't aim to fulfil your hopes for quite a time yet. I'm here as Colonel William S. Granton, late of the Confederate Army. And a highly respected citizen who might open an account at your bank. Supposin', of course, that I think it's a safe place for my money.'

George Cullen recovered some of his poise.

'It's the safest bank in the territory,' he said huffily. 'And an honest one.'

'George, you had a hold-up a few weeks back. And as to bein' honest, how the hell can it be with you runnin' things?'

'Those days are over. For both of us, I hope.'

'They certainly are for me, but I've been hearin' stories from this town. Two fellas was shot in the jailhouse and I was wonderin' why.'

George Cullen shrugged.

'I would imagine that some of the gang didn't want them to go tellin' tales,' he said. 'They looked a pretty tough lot.'

'I'll bet they did,' the visitor agreed softly, 'but they only got away with a few dollars, so I'm told.'

'Four hundred and twenty-four to be exact. I'd locked the safe and hidden the key. Even pretended that I was only a clerk.'

George Cullen looked proud of his achievement and took a sip of the whiskey.

'Good thinking,' Colonel Granton said approvingly. He glanced past the manager's shoulder at the open safe and all the enticing money inside it.

'How much would they have got if they'd cleared you out?' he asked.

'Close on eleven thousand dollars. This is one real prosperous town, you understand.'

'Indeed it is.'

The colonel felt in his pocket and took out a wad of chewing tobacco. He flicked open a large knife and cut himself a slice. He offered it to the manager who shook his head firmly. The colonel thrust the strip into his mouth and chewed at it thoughtfully.

'You were talkin' of makin' a deposit,' George Cullen suggested tentatively.

'So I was, but that was for the benefit of the fellas out there. You and me got a different sort of business to discuss, George. I want some information.'

'Look, Billy, I'm finished with the old days . . .'

The colonel held up a steadying hand.

'Rest easy, fella,' he said soothingly. 'I ain't suggestin' that you and that old coyote behind the counter out there go back to tippin' me off about money shipments. Them days is long gone and we're both too old for wild antics like that. No, all I want is a little bit of information about a gun.'

'A gun!' The manager's mouth dropped open in surprise. 'What sort of gun?'

'One of them old French Lefaucheaux things. It's a .41-calibre pin-fire, and I want to know who the hell in this town still owns one.'

George Cullen relaxed in his chair. The conversation had taken a turn he never expected.

'But they're not used any more,' he said slowly. 'Not since Sam Colt and them other fellas brought in new cartridges and cheap pieces. Why do you want to know?'

Colonel Granton leaned across the desk.

'Let's say it's for old times' sake,' he suggested. 'Don't go all shy on me, George. Just tell me the name of the fella who owns a Lefaucheaux.'

The man shook his head in bewilderment.

'I ain't got the faintest idea,' he said. 'You could ask Wally Payne in the gun store.'

'Oh, sure. And I could go ask the marshal while

I was about it. But I'm askin' an old friend instead. And there's money in it for you, George.'

The bank manager's eyes went a little brighter and he screwed up his face as he thought about the matter.

'It would have to be an older man,' he mused, 'and not a gun-handler in the normal way.'

'It's one of your customers, if that's any help.'

'Are you sure?'

'Certain sure. He lost it in your bank.'

Mr Cullen jerked upright in his seat.

'Good God! Do you mean that it was your family that raided us?'

The colonel smiled and nodded.

'Who's the man, George? I ain't got all day.'

'Well, let's see. The mayor was at the counter. He don't carry nothin' but an old short-barrelled Colt .45. Then Fred Emmet had his .44 Colt. And your kin stole his stickpin as well. He was sure wild about that. Cass Malloy was wearin' a gun. An old thing it were. . . .'

He clicked his fingers. 'That's it. It were Cass Malloy, the saloon-owner. He did have a funny-lookin' piece with a lanyard ring. I always reckoned as how it must have had some sentimental value. Ain't worth a cent as a gun. Just trashy foreign muck. But he likes fancy doodahs like that.'

'Cass Malloy.' The colonel rolled the words

round his tongue. 'Is his the saloon I passed on the main street?'

'Only one in town unless you want to pay high prices at the hotel. Why is this so important, Billy? And where does the money come into it?'

'I can put you in the way of playin' one last little caper in your long and dishonest career, George. Are you interested?'

The money-lender licked his lips uneasily.

'I'm gettin' on in years, Billy. We both are. I can't risk bein' caught and sent to jail. Not at my age.'

Billy Granton grinned.

'No more can I, fella. But there ain't a chance in a hundred of that happenin' if you follow my little scheme. You just have to keep your nerve.'

'I can keep my nerve,' the manager said fiercely, 'but it has to be worth while.'

'Oh, it's worth while, George. You and I simply divide the contents of that safe while you're left lookin' all innocent and virtuous.'

'How?'

'You take all the money home with you one night. Hide your share and wait for me to arrive. I tie you and your wife up like chickens, take your keys and my half of the loot, and then leave all nice and quiet-like. You'll be found in the mornin', the keys will be in the lock of the safe, and you'll be the innocent victim of a gang of bank robbers. It's as easy as that.'

There was a long silence while the bank manager thought it over. Then he slowly shook his head while Billy Granton cut himself another plug of tobacco.

'No, Billy,' he said firmly. 'I don't like it. I'm too old for that sort of thing. Count me out.'

The colonel put the tobacco into his mouth and began to chew slowly.

'That's a shame, George,' he said softly. 'I was hopin' that we could do a little business together for old times' sake. But I reckon you ain't up to it any more. It woulda been a way of makin' amends for the injury you done my family too.'

'Injury? What injury?'

'Well, George, one of them fellas back there in the jailhouse was a nephew of mine. I know you killed him so that he wouldn't go tellin' the court how much money was really took from the bank, Now, I don't like my kin bein' treated like that.'

He suddenly lunged forward across the desk and the large knife buried itself in the centre of the man's chest. George Cullen tried to rise from his chair and scream for help. Only a gurgling sound came from his throat as the colonel's strong hand forced him back into the seat. Then he collapsed, and when the knife was withdrawn, the bank manager slipped gently to the floor.

Billy Granton wiped the weapon on the dead

man's jacket and put it back in his pocket. He looked around the room until he noticed a small straw basket resting by the unlit stove. It contained dry kindling, which he emptied on to the floor.

With a happy smile on his face the colonel started emptying the safe of all the banknotes and coins that he had been eyeing since entering the office. He looked around to make sure that he had missed nothing of value, then let himself out by the back door.

Nobody appeared to take any notice of the distinguished elderly man who rode sedately away from Bluff Point.

TEN

One person had noticed him. The new marshal was standing on the stoop of the jailhouse when Billy Granton came round the corner and entered the bank. A well-dressed stranger with a useful gun at his side was rather an outstanding figure in a small town where folks tended to know each other.

And although there was dust on his boots, his coat was free of travel stains. Jim Clark wondered how the man had got into Bluff Point without coming down the main street. He also wondered where his horse was, and why he had not simply hitched it to the bank's rail for convenience.

The marshal decided to go down the side lane and see if the animal was there out of sight of the main street. He soon found it. A black gelding was tied to a rickety fence a few yards from the back door of the bank. There were saddlebags on the crupper and a dusty trail-coat lay across them. He stroked the animal's back and flanks to see how

94

much it was sweating. It seemed to have been ridden gently but the dust suggested a long journey.

Jim Clark was intrigued enough to go and saddle his own animal and keep it ready behind the jailhouse. He waited for the man to leave by the front door of the bank, and then began to realize that he should be watching the rear of the building. He went to stand on a corner where he could just glimpse the stranger's horse without being seen himself.

The man eventually emerged. He carried a small straw basket and tied it casually to the saddle after donning his trail coat. There was no hurry in his movements as he mounted the horse after checking the cinch. He gently headed the animal for the edge of town. Jim decided to follow at a distance.

Billy Granton rode steadily for a couple of hours. The sun had begun to go down and the shadows were lengthening by the time he reached water. It was a small creek that oozed from higher ground near by. The elderly man unsaddled his horse, let it drink, and lit a small fire near the water. He soon had coffee boiling and a smell of frying bacon wafted on the evening air.

He settled down to feed while Jim Clark watched from some thirty yards away. The marshal was hungry, but did not bother to take any of the bread and cheese from his saddlebag. He was too focused on the man who now sat peacefully by the fire and ate his supper.

The marshal began to think that he was wasting his time and making a fool of himself. He doubted his aroused suspicions and had thoughts of going quietly back to town and forgetting the whole thing. But something intrigued him about the set-up. To go in the front door of the bank and come out of the rear was strange enough, but with a manager like George Cullen, it seemed mighty important. Almost as if the stranger was some sort of accomplice.

Jim sighed heavily as the cold of the night began to make itself felt. Moths were out now, flying round the fire while bats swooped as if from nowhere amid the little sounds that came from the darkness.

Then something happened to alert him again. Billy Granton had finished his meal and cleaned the plate with sand. He now poked the fire to give a better light, and drew the little straw basket towards him. He took out something that made the marshal gasp almost audibly. The old stranger had a handful of banknotes and was starting to count them.

Billy Granton jumped in surprise when a figure with a shotgun loomed out of the blackness. The hammers were pulled back on both barrels and the slim young fellow looked as if he meant business. The gleam of the lawman's badge showed in the firelight as the old man sat with the money in one hand while the other still clasped the little basket.

'You gave an old man a nasty shock, Marshal,' Billy said in as calm a voice as he could muster. 'I thought I was bein' held up for a moment. Come and take a cup of coffee. There's still one left, and you can have a bit of bacon and some beans if you're hungry.'

'Thank you, but I'm nursin' this gun at the moment and I don't seem to have a hand free.' Jim waved the barrel of the gun towards the wad of notes. 'You have quite a parcel of money there.'

'Just drawn it from Bluff Point bank,' Billy said with false cheerfulness. 'Got a big cattle deal to settle and those fellas want cash money. They just won't take cheques and banker's orders. Real suspicious folk they are.'

'Just like me, fella. Now, I suggest that you empty that bag on to the ground, and do it nice and slow. I'm real nervous.'

Billy Granton put down the notes he held and used both hands to turn the little basket upside down so that the rest of the money fell out.

Jim whistled when he saw how much there was.

'You sure as hell cleared out George Cullen's bank,' he said in admiration.

'They had it ready for me,' the old man explained tersely. 'These deals are arranged well in advance.'

Jim moved a few paces nearer until the barrels of the gun were within three or four feet of Billy Granton.

'They even gave you bags of small change,' he said, 'and Mr Cullen put it all in that little basket they use for kindlin' in his office. Now, if that ain't the strangest way of doin' bank business I ever heard tell of. I think you and me is goin' back to town, fella.'

'Now, look here, Marshal—'

'Just stand up nice and slow, keep your right hand above your head, and unbuckle your belt with the other hand. You get it wrong, fella, and I'll let fly.'

Billy Granton knew when he was defeated. He shrugged cheerfully and did as the marshal ordered. His gunbelt slipped to the ground and he stood defenceless in front of the lawman.

'Marshal,' he said as he spread his hands in a gesture of surrender, 'you got me fair and square, and no mistake. But maybe we could do a deal.'

'What happened in the bank?'

Billy shrugged. 'Well, I told the manager fella that I had a lotta money to invest, and he was only too happy to do business. Then it was just a matter of stickin' a gun in his ribs and a gag in his mouth.

He had to sit there all trussed up like a chicken while I emptied the safe. Sweetest little job I ever pulled. But you and me could do a trade. I'm an old man, Marshal, and I don't fancy goin' to jail at my time of life. You've got the money back, and that'll do you a lotta good in town. You could even tell them you'd killed me in a shoot-out.'

'So what have you got to trade?' Jim asked tersely.

'Well, now, why don't we sit down and discuss this over a cup of coffee?'

'We'll stand.'

'As you wish, Marshal. I reckon you're the fella in charge. Now, here's the deal. I've got some information about your town that could solve a crime committed about twenty years ago. The criminal's livin' high on the hog and that bank fella is in it up to the neck. How's that for a start?'

Jim Clark thought about it for a moment. It seemed to be part of the mystery that loomed over Bluff Point and he was curious to solve it.

'If you've got a real, worthwhile tale to tell,' he said slowly, 'I reckon as how you might be able to ride outa here. But your story had better be good.'

'Marshal, I can promise you that it's the prize outa the cracker-barrel. Shall we begin?'

'Start talkin' then.'

Billy Granton lowered his hands carefully and squatted down before the fire. The marshal stood over him, the shotgun still cocked and his eyes alert for any wrong move.

'George Cullen was a clerk in that bank when you were still goin' to the schoolhouse. He was crooked as sin, even in them days. He used to tip off folk like me on any big money movements that he heard about. One of the tips was about a lumber company payroll, but it all went wrong. One of the company fellas managed to get away with the money and me and my kin was left bare-assed and lookin' real foolish. But that lumber company fella didn't go back to his bosses. He took off with the cash and ain't been heard of since. Until now.'

He took out a wad of chewing tobacco and a knife. As he peeled off a slice, he offered it politely to the marshal and then popped it into his own mouth with a long, hard chomping sound.

'The fella settled down in Bluff Point and used the money to set up in business and become a prominent citizen. I got his name, and I reckon that the law enforcement fellas would be mighty pleased to close that case.'

'Who told you who he was? George Cullen?'

'That's right. I figure as how George helped him settle down in Bluff Point. The fella you need to pick up is Cass Malloy, the saloon-owner. He owned a .41 Lefaucheaux pistol when he worked for the lumber company and still owned it till recently. My kin found the cartridge cases where the payroll was took.'

'And that's all you have to offer? An old crime like that ain't of much interest to the courts. And him bein' a friend of pretty important people in town, don't help none.'

Billy grinned as he sliced off more tobacco.

'Oh, I got a little more. You had two fellas in the jailhouse for that bank job. They was shot right under your noses and I figure as how you'd sure as hell like to clear *that* killin' off the books. It don't sit well with law enforcement when the jailhouse ain't safe, do it?'

'Go on.'

'George Cullen shot 'em. They stole just over a hundred dollars but he took another three hundred and blamed them for it. He couldn't have them two fellas goin' before a judge and tellin' their side of the story, could he.'

'Can you prove it?'

'I think so. George always carries a small gun. Somethin' he could tuck away in a pocket. Now, if you or me was to kill a fella, we'd be usin' a .44 or .45. But George Cullen uses a .32. I remember it as a dinky-dainty Hopkins and Allen with all the bluein' rubbed off. You can easily check. I ain't steerin' you wrong.'

'No, you ain't. I've seen him with it.'

'There you are then. The bullets will tell their

tale.' Billy Granton put his head on one side in a knowing way. 'If somebody has had the wit to check the bullets.' He grinned.

'We got the bullets,' Jim lied defensively. 'I reckon you can be on your way now. Saddle up and get the hell outa here. You leave your gun behind and you don't show yourself on my patch again. Understood?'

'As you say, Marshal. You couldn't spare a few dollars eatin' money, I suppose?'

'Get movin' while I'm still feelin' friendly.'

The old man shrugged and got slowly and painfully to his feet. He let out a little groan at the stiffness of his joints and then lunged like lightning at the young man opposite him.

The knife flashed angrily in the firelight as it streaked towards Jim Clark's stomach. The marshal was taken completely off guard and stumbled backwards to trip over the knotted grass and cactus plants. His fingers automatically pulled the triggers and the shotgun blasted off with both barrels.

Birds rose from their sleep and jackrabbits scurried away in a panic. Only a large lizard seemed unmoved by it all as it stared at the dying figure of Billy Granton. It shot its tongue back and forth in its hunt for flying insects that circled in the gunsmoke,

ELEVEN

The Reverend Richard Swann spoke well of the bank manager and led the singing as the casket was lowered into the ground. The whole town had turned out for George Cullen's funeral. It was not a gesture of liking for him, but more the need to console each other for the closing of the bank until further notice, and the effect it would have on local business.

The mayor and old Fred Stales, the chief clerk, had tried to rally people around to lend a little cash so that things could be kept going until money was brought in from another branch. The idea of funding the bank in the meantime was not well received and the building remained closed. A messenger had been sent off to the county seat but it would take a few days for cash to arrive and for a new manager to be appointed.

Jess Bradley paid little attention to the burial service. He had other things on his mind. Not only was the commerce of Bluff Point being disrupted, but the new marshal had also gone missing. The mayor was being blamed for promoting so young and untried a man without consulting the other councillors. He fretted under the heat of the day and was glad when the singing stopped and he could go back to his store.

With his wife holding his arm, Jess turned away from the burial ground and headed for home. There was a cluster of people around, all going for their midday meals now that the entertainment was over. Noisy children were escaping from the schoolhouse and the sound of shovels filling the grave added to the chatter on the street.

'Ain't that young Jim Clark?'

It was the loud voice of Doc Porter that cut in on his thoughts. He looked to where the medical man was pointing and could see the two horses at the far end of the main street. A body lay across one saddle and the other animal was ridden by the lawman. The mayor's face lightened as he quickened his pace to leave his wife behind in his rush to greet the marshal and see what was happening.

The rest of the town seemed to be moving in the same direction, and by the time the lawman neared the jailhouse, he was surrounded by a clamour of questions as people gathered round excitedly.

It was Doc Porter who raised the head of the dead man and let the crowd see who it was. The chief clerk from the bank recognized the late Billy Granton immediately and told everybody that it was the man who had raided the bank and killed George Cullen. He did not feel it wise to tell them that he had once been an informer for the same old rogue.

Jim Clark was not particularly surprised to learn of the manager's death. He had thought about things a little more on his way back to town and come to the conclusion that killing the money lender would have been the easiest way for the bandit to handle the matter.

Mayor Bradley turned to the crowd in high delight. His smile lit up the thin face.

'There you are, folks,' he bawled. 'That's the marshal I appointed, and he's already got the man who robbed our bank. We have ourselves a fine lawman here, and this town is safe in his hands.'

He grabbed Jim Clark by the arm and tried to steer him into the jailhouse while the mortician took over like some eager black vulture. Then the mayor changed his mind. His own whiskey was better than that supplied by the late marshal

Welsby. He ushered Jim Clark through the crowd to his own hardware store opposite.

The marshal was not even given a chance to tend to the two horses as the First Citizen steered him through the doorway and into the privacy of his office. Ma Bradley and a lad were left to mind the store as usual.

'Tell me what's goin' on, fella,' the mayor urged. 'I had to go puttin' up a front for you when the folks found we'd been robbed and that the marshal had done a vanishin' act.'

Jess Bradley listened avidly as Jim told his tale of how he had decided to follow Billy Granton and what had happened. He also confirmed that George Cullen had stolen the $300 and that Billy Granton had given the name of the man who robbed the lumber company twenty years ago. He mentioned the French gun that was involved in the matter.

The mayor's face tautened at the news. His pleasure seemed to have suddenly ebbed away.

'We're gettin' on delicate ground there, lad,' he muttered, 'and it's all one hell of a time past. What name did he give?'

'Cass Malloy.'

The mayor's face seemed to lighten at the news.

'Is that a fact now? Well, he never was a straight sorta fella, so I reckon as how you was steered in the right direction. What do you intend to do?'

Jim Clark felt a little uneasy. Mayor Bradley seemed pleased at the name that emerged. It was almost as though he had expected someone else to be exposed. The young marshal decided to play things cautiously.

'I'll wait and see if any more evidence turns up,' he said quietly. 'After all, it's only the word of a bank robber tryin' to cut himself a deal, and a hell of a lot of years have passed. Just like you said, Mr Mayor.'

'Yeah, yeah, of course.' Jess Bradley seemed almost disappointed. 'I guess that's the right thing to do. And you're sure about George Cullen shootin' the two prisoners?'

'I'm gonna check that as well.'

'Good for you, lad. I have a feelin' that things will settle down nicely in this town with you as the lawman.'

Neither of them had noticed that Mrs Bradley was listening at the door. She was a woman who did not like to be left out of the latest gossip, and this was as hot as a sizzling skillet. As the two men settled down for a quiet drink, she left the lad to mind the store and hurried along the street to spread the word to her friends.

It was about half an hour later when Jim Clark called on Doc Porter. The medical man had just finished lunch and was in his large office, slightly flushed and smelling of whiskey.

'Did I take the bullets out of them two bandit fellas" he bawled. 'Why the hell would I do a thing like that? They was dead. All I did was check their pulses and hand them over for burial.'

He glanced at the marshal over his spectacles.

'What does it matter, anyways?' he asked as curiosity took over.

'It might tell me who killed them, Doc,' Jim told him.

He left the medico to work it out while he went along the street to where the funeral parlour sat a little way back from the main drag. Les Jenkins was in the back room doing something probably unpleasant and came out to greet the new marshal. He tried to smile but it was only the caricature he gave to bereaved relatives. Just a display of large teeth that would have made good tombstones.

'And what can I do for you, lad?' he asked. 'Or should I call you a marshal these days?'

'Those two fellas who were shot in the jailhouse,' Jim said quietly. 'Did you remove the bullets from their bodies?'

The mortician's formal smile vanished as he looked at the young man with a new expression. It was one of respect.

'I did indeed,' he said. 'Why do you ask?'

'I'm tryin' to find out who killed them.'

'I see. It was the popular notion at the time that their own friends did it to stop them talkin' to the law.'

Jim caught a certain something in the man's voice. 'And you didn't agree, Mr Jenkins?'

'No. They was shot with .32-calibre bullets, and folks who go around robbin' banks don't carry dinky little pieces like that. I've got the bullets if you want them.'

Jim shook his head. 'It don't matter now,' he said. 'You've told me who did the shootin'. Why didn't you mention it to Marshal Welsby at the time?'

The man grinned. A real attempt this time.

'Ethan just wanted a quiet life, and I reckon as how he'd have laughed at me. You're different, young fella. You'll make a good lawman, and we sure need one.'

Jim Clark left the mortician's office with a spring in his step. He had at least solved one problem and had also established himself in the eyes of the community. He walked slowly back to the jailhouse and took little notice of the thick-set man who was striding down the main street.

Cass Malloy's face was a picture of suppressed rage. The owner of the Lady Luck saloon was a tough-looking character who was capable of dealing with the roughest drunk and who was never known to shirk a fight of any sort. He carried a gun at his side and his frock-coat was pulled back by his right hand so that the weapon was ready to draw. He stopped in mid-stride when he saw the marshal approaching and bawled at him.

'You got me called a payroll thief all round town!' he bellowed. 'A wet-behind-the-ears kid goes tellin' folks that I'm a hold-up man. You sure got one hell of a nerve, young fella. You'd better draw because I'm takin' that from nobody, marshal or no marshal.'

The people in the street stopped in their tracks to listen to the words. Then they began to realize the danger and scattered into the various buildings.

Jim Clark raised a hand to try and stop the enraged saloon owner in his stride. He shouted a few words but they were drowned by the man's angry tirade as he neared the marshal. Cass Malloy was beyond reason and his hand flew to the butt of the gun at his side. He drew it smoothly, and the sound of the hammer coming back was loud in the silent street.

Jim had no choice. He dropped his own hand to the .44 on his hip. He was younger and faster. The two pistols exploded almost at the same moment and Cass Malloy staggered back a few steps. He raised his gun and fired again, but his second shot smashed a window in one of the stores. Then he sank to his knees and slowly collapsed on his face.

The young lawman breathed a sigh of relief. His reaction had been automatic and he did not even know how he had managed to shoot so accurately. His hand was trembling as he holstered the gun and approached the fallen man. Blood oozed from Cass Malloy's back to show that the piece of lead had gone right through. He was quite dead.

A crowd began to gather round. Nobody knew quite what to say to the lawman. The saloon-owner was not popular but the grounds for the quarrel were not understood and there were furtive looks on the faces of the townsfolk as they watched the doctor arrive and examine the body. The mortician was not far behind on such a profitable occasion.

Jim found somebody tugging his arm. He turned to face the mayor, who seemed rather pleased with events.

'You did a good job there, young fella,' he said. 'Come and have a drink while Les Jenkins clears up. I reckon we've got ourselves the man what robbed the payroll all them years ago.'

He ushered the young marshal into the hardware store and poured out a measure of his best imported whiskey.

An hour or so later Wally Payne paid a call on the mayor. He took him aside to a corner of the store where they could not be overheard.

'Your wife's got it goin' all round town that Cass Malloy was the fella what robbed the lumber payroll,' he whispered urgently. 'You and me both knows that he ain't.'

The mayor waved a dismissive hand.

'That don't matter a damn, Wally,' he replied angrily. 'Cass Malloy was a no-good and he'll fit the bill nicely. It closes the whole business and lets us live in peace.'

'Does it hell!' the gun-store owner snapped. 'You and I both know that it's all to do with that foreign gun. Wally Payne bought that off me, and we both know where I got it. Suppose his wife opens her mouth?'

Jeff Bradley thought about it for a moment.

'George Cullen seems to have named Cass Malloy. He must have noticed Cass wearin' the gun and told that Billy Granton fella. It seems that Cullen was once mixed up with the old rogue, and he talked to young Jim Clark before they had a shoot-out.'

'And what did the old fella want the information for?' Wally asked. 'Did he have some connection with that woman and the fella that shot Marshal Welsby? We could have ourselves trouble here, Jeff. What are we gonna do?'

'Cass Malloy's wife won't run a saloon,' the mayor said thoughtfully.'I offered him a fair price a coupla years back, but he tried to hold me to ransom. I'll do a deal with her and she can go live some place else. The money will keep her mouth shut.'

'I hope you're right, but somebody else might talk and there'll be more killin' trouble for all of us.'

TWELVE

The young man who wandered about town was quietly spoken, well behaved, and dressed like a preacher or lawyer. He had dark hair, no gun, and was lodging at Ma Braddock's boarding-house. She told her friends that he was a schoolmaster passing through to a job up north. He listened quietly to what she had to tell him about life in Bluff Point, and went for a few drinks to the saloon where he picked up more gossip.

He saw Marshal Clark bring back the body of Billy Granton and was among the folk who ducked for cover when the lawman shot Cass Malloy. Soon after that event he left town amid a few friendly waves and smiles from people who regarded him as a regular sort of fellow.

If anybody had noticed, he was not travelling north towards his new job, but almost due west where he eventually ended up at the mouth of a small gully.

The cabin at the far end of this forsaken place was a miserable-looking building with a turf roof that let in as much light as the unglazed window. The creek that flowed nearby was bitter and stained from the rocks over which it flowed. There was a bit of pasture for horses and a small corral that kept them from straying among the poisonous weeds which flourished as a home for tarantulas and scorpions.

Smoke rose from an iron stovepipe and there was a smell of cooking to show that somebody was at home. The Granton gang had fallen on hard times as far as accommodation was concerned. The only consolation was that the place was as safe as they could hope to get.

A miner had built it thirty years ago and dwelt there until the gold in the creek was exhausted. He had drunk himself to death on what little fortune he had made and was still buried under a small mound. The place had been forgotten by every-body but Billy Granton and his friends and family, who had used it on several occasions when things were desperate.

The dark-haired young man drew rein outside the cabin and alighted wearily from his small mare. Phil Granton's disguise had been a good one, and it was not for nothing that he was accepted as the brains of the family. The coffee-stained hair had been his mother's idea though, and had worked well.

Ma Granton came out of the cabin followed by Alf and Tom. The two men helped him to unsaddle the horse and lead it to the corral. Then they hurried inside to hear the news he brought. They all sat around the table as he swallowed some hot coffee.

'Well, why the devil have you taken so long?' Alf asked anxiously, 'and where's Uncle Billy?'

'He's dead, Pa,' Phil told him quietly, 'and he made a complete mess of everythin' we set out to do.'

Alf cursed luridly.

'I mighta known it,' he growled. 'The old fool was past it. Damn near in his dotage.'

'It weren't that, Pa. He just got too greedy.'

Phil told the story of how the old man had robbed the bank, got himself killed by the marshal, and disclosed the name of the man who owned the Lefaucheaux pistol. He too was dead and all their hope of profit had vanished.

'So we get nothin' out of it,' Alf sighed. 'Everythin' was a waste of time.'

Phil grinned and leaned across the table.

'Not quite, Pa,' he said in confident tones. 'We got ourselves a real winner if we move fast.'

Ma Granton poured some more coffee and

reached under the table for the corn-mash jug.

'What you got in mind, lad?' she asked cautiously. 'You sure as hell looks like you swallowed the cream off the milk.'

'I talked to Uncle Billy before he left for town, and he told me somethin' real useful. When he killed old man Cullen and lifted all that money from the bank, they had to close up.' Phil looked round at their puzzled faces. 'There's no telegraph in that town and the mayor had to send a rider to the county seat to tell them what had happened and to have more cash delivered to reopen the bank.'

'So?' Alf asked.

'That means that the money will be on the way to Bluff Point any time now. They got no way of lettin' the county seat know that they killed the bank robber and got it all back. Don't you see? There's a few thousand dollars on its way and we know the route it'll have to take and where it's heading. Easy pickin's for us, Pa.'

Alf Granton scratched the side of his face noisily. He got up to move restlessly round the little room.

'How do we know all this?' he asked. 'I reckon as how they didn't put it up on the church noticeboard.'

'Uncle Billy told me that old Fred Stales was still a clerk at that bank in Bluff Point. So I got in touch with him. It cost every dollar I had on me, but he talked. And I had to promise another five hundred when we get the money.'

'You done well, boy.' Alf's voice was more cheerful than it had been for weeks. 'Can we reach the stage in time?'

'It ain't comin' by stage, Pa. The banks are gettin' wary of usin' regular means. They got themselves a new idea now. It's slower than the stage, but that's all the better for us. We've got one hell of a fast ride if we're gonna reach a good hold-up point ahead of that shipment.'

Alf Granton's eyes gleamed with excitement.

'And old Fred Stales gave you the route?' he urged.

'Sure did, Pa, and drew a map for me.'

Phil pulled a stained piece of thick paper from his pocket and laid it on the table. They all pored over the roughly drawn sketch of the territory and the way the bank money was likely to travel. At last Alf Granton put a grubby finger on a spot that seemed the best place to attack.

'Right there,' he said firmly.

'But, Pa,' Phil protested, 'there ain't no cover and there's only three of us now. We couldn't stop the rig on open ground if it was well guarded. We gotta have cover of some sort.'

'There's four of us,' Ma Granton said grimly.

'You're outa this, Ma,' her husband objected. 'We can't have a rig delayin' us at a time like this.'

'I can ride a horse as well as any man here,' ma protested, 'and ride it astride.'

'That ain't womanly, Ma,' Tom objected. 'No lady ever rides astride 'cept in them tourin' shows. And they ain't decent.'

'I ain't no lady, son. I married into a family of thieves and killers, and my own pa was as crooked as any politician. This is a family business and we all do what has to be done.'

Ma Granton was not an easy woman to argue with and even her husband was not anxious to find himself on the sharp edge of her tongue – or her fist.

'Now, let's plan this all out neat and proper,' Alf said as he pored over the map. 'We gotta reach this point before the rig and then wait patiently. We'll be movin' faster than they can and they ain't likely to travel at night.'

'Is it safe for us to move at night, Pa?' Tom asked. 'We could get ourselves lost. I once did.'

'Son, you could get lost findin' the privy,' Ma said unkindly. 'Your pa knows this territory from way back and he ain't like to lose hisself when there's money to be had.'

They all laughed even though Tom's contribution was a little forced.

'Right,' said Alf after they had discussed the matter a little more, 'we set off tonight as soon as the moon rises, and when we comes back here, we comes back rich.'

*

A wide creek cut across a small area of lush pasture. There were plenty of bushes and wind-bent trees that gave shade to the Granton gang as they sheltered from the hot sun. The sky was cloudless and a slight breeze swayed the grass and rippled the clear water.

Tom had the keenest eyesight and had been hoisted up into the branches of one of the trees to scan the land to the east. That was where the county seat lay on either side of the railroad and where the small rig would come from with the money.

'I reckon we're in good time,' Alf said lazily as he and Phil sat at the base of the tree. 'Them folks will stop here to eat and water the horses. It's an ideal spot and we'll be well hid in all these bushes.'

'You thought it all out well, Pa,' Phil said admiringly.

'Experience, son. And I hope you got things right and they really do come this way.'

'That's what Fred Stales said, Pa. It's a two-horse wagon that's deliverin' farm tools to hardware stores round the county. There'll be two fellas on the rig and another two ridin' somewhere close by. They're travellin' as ranch hands just movin' in the same direction. Them Pinkerton people have

120

organized it, and they're reckoned to be a pretty tough bunch.'

'We can tackle four fellas if they're taken by surprise. A few blasts from shotguns and that cash will be in our pockets.'

'How long do you figure we'll have to wait, Pa?' Tom shouted down from his uncomfortable perch.

'Well, there ain't been nobody near this water-hole in the last week or so, so we ain't missed them. As I work it out, with the speed we travelled and the speed a rig moves, we got maybe till this time tomorrow,' Alf said confidently.

'Then why in hell am I sittin' up here?' Tom bawled.

' 'cos we ain't takin' no chances of bein' wrong. You just sit tight and look for signs of dust.'

Alf's guess was right. It was nearly noon the next day when a haze appeared on the horizon and Tom shouted down to the others. They scanned the distance carefully. After half an hour or so the clear outline of a two-horse wagon and two outriders could be seen heading for the creek.

Tom got himself down from the branch and the three men made sure that their horses were well hidden behind some more distant trees and that their little fire was out and no smoke would give away their location. Guns were checked and they took up positions among the tall grasses and waving shrubs. They had persuaded ma to stay at home and she had reluctantly done so.

Alf had worked everything out and each man knew what he had to do when the money-carriers arrived at the creek to stop for a noon meal. They waited patiently amid the noise of crickets and the hum of buzzing insects.

Alf peered between the dusty branches of some low bushes and watched the wagon draw up alongside the creek. It was covered by a canvas hood which was stretched over iron loops and advertised Johnson's Hardware Supplies. It also boasted that Mr Johnson was a contractor to the United States Army and announced in smaller lettering that he sold Imperial stoves with express delivery.

The two horsemen who rode behind the rig were just about to dismount when Alf raised the shotgun to his shoulder. He let fly with both barrels at the driver and the other man on the wagon. His two sons opened fire at the same moment and the men on horseback tumbled from their mounts.

The horses reared in panic. The mules pulling the wagon careered into each other and dragged the rig into the creek where it lurched over to one side while the animals struggled to keep their footing in the mud. The driver had already fallen from his seat while his companion had half-raised his own shotgun instinctively as he slipped down between the mules and got trampled.

There was a sudden lull as the smoke curled into the sky and the mules and horses quietened down again. Four dead men lay on ground and the acrid smell of powder hung in the air.

'I reckon we got ourselves a few dollars spendin' money,' Alf said cheerfully as he stood up and reloaded the shotgun. 'Let's take a look at what's hidden under all them forks and spades.'

His two grinning sons helped to bring the mules back to dry land before securing the riderless horses and letting them drink peacefully at the creek. They unfastened the ropes that held the rear canvas flaps together, and Phil climbed up on to the rig. There were coils of barbed wire, bundles of spades and shovels, and a collection of oil lamps. Phil moved some canvas bags of nails and let out a little cry of delight as he pulled out a small leather case and waved it in triumph. He passed it down to the eager Alf and the two sons watched as their father broke the little brass lock.

He tipped the mass of papers on to the ground and ran his hand through them with increasing despair. There was no money. Just a collection of bank statements, exchange notes, and cancelled cheques. They searched the rig for another hour and then turned their attention to the dead men. Their efforts resulted in a total of fifteen dollars and a couple of silver watches. Everything had been a waste of time.

THIRTEEN

The stage arrived at the usual time and a few passengers alighted on to the main street of Bluff Point. They were all passing through and would only take an hour or so to rest and eat while the horses were changed for the journey on to the next stop at Leamington.

The mayor and the marshal stood at the door of the Wells Fargo office and scanned the new arrivals anxiously. The man they were looking for was easy to miss in a crowd. He was small and stooped, seemed to be at least fifty, and stared short-sightedly around through gold-rimmed spectacles. They hid the keeness of his dark eyes and only a close observer would have noticed another man who had also alighted and stood discreetly in the background.

He was also easy to miss in a bunch, but there was a gun at his waist and his heavy figure looked as if it would be handy in a fight. They were both

Pinkerton agents and the little man carried the money to replace that which had been stolen by Uncle Billy Granton. It was in a small carpetbag which he was carrying; it seemed of so little importance that he put it on the ground while he dusted the lapels of his suit and wiped his face with a large bandanna. He looked rather vacantly at the mayor as the First Citizen approached.

'Mr Evans?' he greeted the man. 'I'm Mayor Bradley and this is our marshal, Jim Clark. I hope you had a good journey.'

'As rattlin' and dusty as ever was,' the little man snapped. 'But we got here safe and I reckon that's all that matters. Where's the bank?'

'I'll take you there,' the mayor said as he watched Mr Evans pick up the carpetbag again. 'There is just one little problem that has arisen, however. We got the stolen money back again. The marshal here took care of the bank robber and every cent has been recovered.'

They were now on their way across the street and the little man stopped in his tracks.

'I've travelled eighty miles or more in that damned rackety bone-shaker and it weren't necessary?' he whined angrily. 'Well, that sure beats all. Dave and me gotta go on to Leamington for another assignment, and we could have got there by railroad if we'd been told.'

'I'm afraid that's the case, Mr Evans,' Mayor

Bradley said apologetically. 'But we've got no tele-graph here and you'd left the county seat before we could send another messenger. What will you do with the money now?'

'Do what I was ordered to do. I'll deliver it to the chief clerk and he can make what arrangements he likes. I gotta get back on that stage and head for the next job.'

He looked ahead, spotted the sign in the window of the bank and headed purposefully in that direction. Jim and the mayor followed meekly.

Fred Stales welcomed them effusively and they were all led into the manager's office. The money was taken out of the carpetbag to be carefully checked and signed for. They watched old Fred put it in the safe and then all took a drink of whiskey as though in celebration of a job well done.

Mr Evans produced a letter from his pocket, which he passed over to the chief clerk. Fred tore the envelope open eagerly.

'I guess this is my official appointment as manager,' he told his visitors. His hands trembled slightly at the thought as he read the letter care-fully. His expression changed after a moment or two and he cursed softly before throwing the missive down on the desk.

'They're sendin' a new manager,' he moaned angrily. 'I ain't good enough for them after thirty years or more service. Too old, I suppose, and they'll put some whipper-snapper in the place I should have had.'

The three visitors left him to his bad mood and crossed to the saloon where they had something to eat and drink. Mr Evans got back on the stage, still shadowed by his discreet colleague, and the mayor shook hands again and wished him a safe journey.

'You need the telegraph in this town,' Mr Evans said as a parting shot. 'And the railroad. You'll never amount to a row of beans until you get one or the other.'

Mayor Bradley swallowed his pride and agreed politely as he waved the man off on his next assignment. He turned thankfully to Jim Clark with relief clearly written on his face.

'Well, it's all over,' he said happily. 'We've saved the bank, got rid of the man who robbed the lumber company all them years ago, and started your career off on the right foot, young fella. We even know that George Cullen killed them two prisoners. So, no more problems, Jim, and that's how I want to keep it.'

The new marshal nodded a silent agreement. He did not bother to tell the mayor that he had recently had a long talk with Mrs Malloy, and that the saloon keeper's widow had been very helpful.

He approached her rather cautiously. After all, he

had shot her husband and he was not sure how he would be received. One of the things that gave him confidence was the fact that she had kept the saloon open during all her troubles and did not seem particularly upset at the funeral. She was a tall, straight woman with a pinched face and firm mouth. Rumour had it that she was not happily married. On that basis he asked the head bartender if he could have a quiet word with her.

The private rooms above the Lady Luck saloon were plainly furnished. It was not Jim Clark's idea of the home of a successful businessman, but the impression was one of austerity. Mrs Malloy seemed suited to the room to which she admitted the young lawman.

She invited him to be seated while she poured coffee as though they were at some church meeting of the Christian Ladies' Guild. There was a large organ in one corner, its mirrors reflecting the daylight and its candle-holders' plain pewter to match the dull covers of the hymn-books that sat on the little shelves.

'I'm sorry about Mr Malloy,' Jim started tentatively, 'but I had no—'

'Landsakes, Marshal, I'm not blaming you for the evil temper of a hot-headed man who will probably be quarreling with Satan at this very minute. I'm a Christian woman, Marshal, but I cannot deny that Mr Malloy was not an easy man.

You had to defend yourself and I know that he intended to kill you.'

She handed over a cup of coffee and sat straight in her chair with large-knuckled hands folded on her lap.

'But he was not the man who robbed the lumber company,' she said sternly. 'You got it all wrong there, Marshal. My husband started life as a gambling man, and we came to this town with the winnings he'd taken from poor fools who didn't know a cheating rogue when they saw one. He used that money to start the saloon here, and we made a good living out of it. I found the Lord some years back, but he never mended his ways. I've had to live with that. And that's the truth. I'll be selling this place now and spending the rest of my life doing the Lord's work.'

'And the foreign gun, Mrs Malloy?' Jim asked. 'That was the main thing that seemed to identify him.'

The woman's head swivelled to a bare patch on the wall.

'There used to be a glass case there,' she said with firm disapproval. 'Cass had a collection of old guns. He liked the things and bought that particular one right here in town. I made him put them away. They're ungodly works to be hanging up in a Christian home.'

'Where did he buy it, Mrs Malloy?' Jim thought

that he already knew the answer.

'He got it off Wally Payne,' she replied, 'and liked it so much that he took to wearing it most of the time. He was real put out when those bank robbers took it from him. Real put out he was and mean-tempered for days after. You have a word with Wally Payne. He deals in the evil things.'

'I'll do that, Mrs Malloy.'

He talked to Wally less than an hour later. The store was free of customers at the time and the man looked a little surprised to see the new marshal.

'And what can I do for you, Jim?' he asked cheerfully. Jim sensed that the lanky man was not at ease and he leaned over the counter to stare hard at the large-nosed features of the gun–dealer.

'I shot a coupla fellas recently, as you well know, Wally,' he said slowly. 'Ain't a thing I like doin' but my job calls for a bit of killin' now and then.'

'You've been doin' a good job, Marshal.' The man's voice had a slight quaver. 'We need a tough lawman.'

'But I like to shoot the right fellas, Wally, and I gets mighty upset if people give me a wrong steer and I shoot an innocent man. Understand what I mean?'

'Can't say as I rightly do, Marshal,' Wally Payne said, licking his dry lips. 'What exactly is you on about?'

'I was told that Cass Malloy owned the gun that was used by the fella what went off with a lumber company payroll. A foreign piece it was. .41 calibre. Was I told right?'

Wally Payne was sweating and one little bead of moisture fell off his large nose as he shook his head violently.

'I don't rightly know what we're on about here, Jim,' he said weakly. 'I reckon as how you should talk to the mayor.'

'Oh, I will. But right now I'm talkin' to you, and if I don't get the truth, I might just bounce this gun of mine off your thick skull. You gotta work with the law, Wally, or you could end up in my jailhouse. So tell me about Cass Malloy's gun.'

'I gotta live in this town, Jim,' the gun-dealer whined, 'and there are folk here I don't aim to offend. You know how things are in a small place like Bluff Point.'

'Talk, Wally. I don't have to repeat what you tell me.'

The man stood in silence for a moment and then slowly nodded his head.

'Let's go into the back room,' he said. 'The lad can look after the store.'

After calling his apprentice from the workshop, Wally Payne led the marshal into a comfortable room where he offered a glass of whiskey before sitting down and gesturing the lawman to do the same. Jim Clark refused the drink but sat watching as the gun-dealer swallowed his in one shot.

'Mayor Bradley brought me the gun,' he said as he wiped his lips. 'It was a lotta years ago, and he said that he was sellin' it for a friend. It weren't worth much because the Union army had sold thousands of them after the war. They was real old-fashioned. I gave him a few dollars, and when Cass Malloy saw it on show, he was right eager to buy it. Paid a decent price too. He'd bought a few unusual guns from me. Had quite a collection of them, though I hear tell that his sour-faced wife don't like the idea.'

'Could it have been used by the fella from the lumber company?'

Wally nodded slowly.

'I guess so. Same calibre, accordin' to the mayor's wife. She sure heard you and him talkin' about it, and the tale was all around town in no time. There was nothin' I could do.'

'You could have tried, Wally.'

The man shook his head. 'It all happened too fast. I don't know where the mayor got that gun, and if you wants to know, go ask him. But we'll be needin' a new marshal if you do.'

There was a long silence. Eventually Jim Clark rose to his feet. He felt that he had got as much information as he was likely to get, and that the mayor was the only one who knew the whole story.

He was a bit surprised when Wally Payne decided to say something else.

'Look, Jim,' the man said softly. 'The fella that owned that gun and went off with the cash was young and maybe a mite foolish. We all are when we're turned loose with a livin' to make. Things was wilder in them days, and as a man ages, he regrets the past. Wants to live a better life. It was all a long time ago. Why not let it lie?'

'I got a feelin' that there's one hell of a lot of coverin'-up goin' on in this town. Why in blazes is the mayor protectin' a bandit? In case you don't know the whole story as I've pieced it together, he took off with all the money.'

Wally Payne nodded and almost managed a grin.

'He sure as hell did,' he agreed, 'and he ended up in this town, Jim. And became one right good citizen, so I'm told. I don't know who he is but some of the councilmen do, and maybe the preacher and the judge are in on it. But they all reckon him for a good man. And why not? After all, he gave back the money.'

FOURTEEN

Fred Stales packed his bags and left town on an old mule. Nobody cared. Least of all the other clerks in the bank where he had worked. His sour old face and spoken ambition to be the new manager had only made him more enemies, and the two younger clerks were glad to see him go.

But Fred was a vengeful man. He had known Billy Granton for many years and, like the late manager, had earned a few dollars for passing information to him now and then. He had more information now and his furtive meeting with young Phil had left him with the knowledge of where the Granton family could be found.

The hold-up had gone wrong and the cash had arrived by a different route. But that was not Fred's fault. He had done his best and now had a way to put things right and earn himself a real slice of ready cash. He travelled for the best part of two days to the little cabin where the Grantons were now living.

His welcome was not a happy one and it was difficult to stop Alf killing him then and there. Only the old man's pleas and the intervention of the more level-headed Phil saved Fred Stales to tell his tale.

He explained how the mayor was boasting about a letter he had sent to the county seat with the man who carried details of the bank's troubles. It had probably been a warning to have a decoy rig on the move while the money reached Bluff Point in some other way. The money had now turned up safely.

Alf listened in frustrated silence and eventually admitted that there was nothing that Fred could have done about it.

'Well, I reckon that finishes us in that gopher hole of a town,' he said glumly. 'The fella who owned the gun is dead, George Cullen is dead, and we lost a chance at robbin' the bank. There don't seem a hope in hell of makin' a bent cent outa that damned place.'

A sly grin spread over Fred Stales's face. This was what he had been waiting for.

'You ain't finished yet, Alf,' he said eagerly. 'How would you and the lads like to pick up fifteen thousand dollars?'

'Sure. We'll stage a raid on the Washington

mint. What the blazes is you talkin' about, Fred Stales?'

'I know a bank that has about fifteen thousand dollars tucked away in its safe. And the marshal is goin' to leave town soon to see what happened to that rig you held up. He'll have to when it don't arrive.'

He looked round at the four faces in the cabin and found a quiet satisfaction at their puzzlement.

'What the hell is you on about?' Ma Granton asked as she laid the enamel coffee-pot on the table.

'The bank got back the money that your Uncle Billy took. But they'd already sent off for help to the head office at the county seat. That money has arrived and it's now in Bluff Point. Them Pinkerton fellas who brought it in had to go to another job some place else. So it's gonna stay in that safe until the folks at head office can make arrangements to collect it again. My bank is holdin' more money than any place in the territory.'

'Fifteen thousand dollars.' Alf breathed the words as though they were part of a prayer.

'But Bluff Point,' said Ma doubtfully. 'We've already tangled up there, fella.'

'The marshal's a whipper-snapper, and he has to leave town to look for that rig sooner or later. He'll take a few other fellas with him, and they'll likely be the best gun-handlers in town. The place would be wide open.'

It was Phil who spoke next. He had been silently thinking about the situation.

'Suppose the safe is locked, like it was last time we paid your bank a visit?'

Fred Stales took a bunch of keys out of his pocket.

'Then you just open it up,' he said cheerfully.

They all exchanged broad smiles and Ma Granton picked up the keys to hug them to her ample bosom.

'Then it all depends on the marshal takin' a ride outa town,' she crooned.

And so he did. Jim Clark and the mayor fretted over the failure of the decoy rig to reach Bluff Point. It was eventually decided that the new marshal should take a small posse to try and back-trail the wagon until they found what had gone wrong.

There were few takers for the job but three men eventually volunteered to ride out in the searing heat to find the lost rig and its occupants.

Bluff Point was left a quiet and contented place with the bank being run by the two remaining clerks and everything going its usual dull way. Mayor Bradley was having private talks with Mrs Malloy about taking over the saloon; the mortician was anticipating a few more burials; and Preacher

Swann was preparing a long sermon for Sunday. It was to be about how the Almighty had saved the town from the Granton gang.

Saturday night passed without incident. The local ranches paid their hands once a month and there was still another week to go before the thirsty wranglers came into town to spend their wages. The town folk drank quietly and went home at reasonable times. Lights began to go out in the houses and the main street became the haunt of scavenging rats and diving owls that hunted for food.

The four men who came down the dark side-lane and tethered their mounts behind the bank were never noticed. They dismounted silently and Fred Stales opened the back door with trembling fingers. He had not wanted to come with them, but Alf Granton trusted nobody. If there was any sort of trap, he was going to make sure that the bank clerk got his share of the flying lead.

They moved quietly down the passage on floorboards that creaked under their weight. The door of the manager's office was not even locked, and they were standing in front of the large safe with slightly unbelieving looks on their faces. They could hardly see each other in the darkness, but all felt the same as Phil and Alf touched the cold steel of the safe door as though they were caressing a woman.

They could hear Fred Stales breathing heavily as

he struggled to find the right key on the bunch. His fingers moved across the surface of the door to locate the keyhole and they heard rather than saw him move the cover aside. The door swung slowly back as he tugged with gasping breath. A slight smell of stale air came wafting out at them from the interior of the safe.

Alf reached into his shirt for the cotton bags that were ready to house the loot. He handed one to Phil and another to Tom.

'Let's have some light here,' he whispered. 'Are there blinds on this place?'

'The window's frosted,' Fred Stales whispered back, 'and the only house behind us is the preacher's place. He'll be abed at this time of the night, so I reckon we're safe. But just a vesta and no more, Alf.'

They could hear the rattle of the vesta-case in the darkness as Alf extracted a match and struck it on the silver grating. The sudden flare lit up the place and Phil cursed as he cupped his hands round the flame and stood as close to his father as he could. Their shadows danced on the wall as they peered at the money that lay before them in the safe. Tom and Fred hurriedly scooped the notes into the gaping bags while Alf and Phil made sure that the flame shone only towards the safe to light up the scene of action.

But Preacher Swann was not in bed. His long

sermon was giving him problems and he had wandered out of the living-room to stand in the kitchen with a glass of water in his hand. He stared out at the night sky and thought about the words he wanted to utter the next day. His finely chiselled face was in repose as he considered the years he had spent in Bluff Point and the good work he had managed to do. It was a nice place to live, to bring up children, and a town in which he was loved and respected by all.

The sudden flicker of light took him by surprise. It was almost as though it were some trick of his eyes, and he blinked as he stared through the glass. His breath steamed up the window and he wiped away the moisture to peer at the back wall of the bank across the alley. There were slight shadows behind the frosted glass of the office window and he looked up and down the alley as far as his range of vision would permit. There was no moon but he could make out the shapes of several horses tied to the rail of the corral down to his left.

Richard Swann was not a cowardly man, but he was a man of peace and his first instinct was to go and get the marshal. Then he remembered that the lawman was out of town searching for the missing decoy rig. The preacher put down the glass tumbler, left the kitchen and went back to the living-room where his old Winchester sat over the lintel of the door. He took it down and checked the load. His wife and three children were in bed and he left the house quietly to go across the main street and rouse the mayor.

He ran round to the back door of the hardware store and only had to knock once to be admitted. Mayor Bradley was in his slippers, smoking a stogie, and with a book in his hand. He put the rather lurid novelette behind his back when he saw who his guest was.

'We gotta get some help, Preacher,' he said when the problem was explained. 'You go rouse Wally Payne and Les Hutton while I fetch my gun. If the horses are at the rear of the bank, that's where we'll lie for them.'

The preacher ran off to warn the other two men while Mayor Bradley took out his shotgun, loaded it, and set out across the main street to go down the back lane where the rear door of the bank was located. He saw the four tethered horses, and noticed the slight shadows at the window of the office. Preacher Swann had not been having some sort of illusion. There was somebody in the bank. Jess Bradley quietly untied the horses and led them away.

As he tethered them to another rail at the side of the livery stable, his colleagues arrived, each armed with carbines and with the gun-store owner wearing a pair of .44 Colts at his waist.

The four men moved quietly down the narrow

lane until they reached the rear of the bank. They were almost too late. The door was open and three men were emerging stealthily. Wally Payne did not wait for orders, he raised his carbine and fired

Nobody was quite sure what happened next. The three figures vanished again, pushing their way back into the bank and slamming the door behind them. The window of the manager's office suddenly shattered and several shots were fired at the mayor and his posse.

They ducked for cover and only Jess Bradley managed to get off both barrels of his shotgun as he crouched behind a rain barrel. Then there was a silence as Wally Payne nudged the preacher at his side.

'I reckon we ain't the knowinest lawmen in the business,' he said in a rueful tone. 'Them fellas is out the front door by now and well gone.'

The mayor cheered up at the thought and rose slowly to his feet.

'Well, we did our best,' he said. 'So who the hell were they?'

The preacher had not waited for the answer to that question. He ran back to the main street and poked his head round the corner to get a glimpse of the bank's front door. It was wide open and he could see three figures running wildly towards the livery stable. One of them shouted something and pointed. They had seen the tethered horses and were mounting before Richard Swann could cock the carbine and get a bead on one of them.

He fired, but they were already in motion and heading out of town. By the time he was joined by the mayor and the gun dealer, the main street was empty.

'Well, I reckon we've lost every cent in the bank,' Mayor Bradley said wearily as he stood in the middle of the street. 'I suppose we did our best, but marshals we ain't.'

'We'd better check the safe,' Preacher Swann suggested. 'They might have been disturbed before they could open it.'

The mayor brightened up.

'That's surely a thought,' he said. 'There weren't no noise of blastin' powder.'

He led the way through the open door of the building and walked through to the office at the back. Wally Payne struck a vesta and lit the overhead oil-lamp. It threw a warm but disappointing glow over the little room. The safe door stood wide open and there was no money to be seen.

The mayor started to curse but remembered that the preacher was there. Faces were now staring in at the shattered window and people were entering the bank from the main street. Once the shooting had stopped the townsfolk grew brave enough to venture out. The two clerks appeared on the scene and surveyed the damage.

'They didn't break in,' one of them said softly. 'They used keys.'

He pointed to the bunch that still hung from the keyhole of the safe door. Mayor Bradley took them out and weighed them in his hand.

'Whose keys?' he asked tautly.

The other clerk waved his own bunch in the mayoral face.

'They sure as hell ain't mine,' he said, 'but I figure as how Fred Stales had copies made and took them with him. He's gotta be behind this. There ain't no other set outside head office.'

'Why didn't you get the keys offen him then?' the mayor stormed.

'We didn't know he had them, and we didn't know he was leaving,' the clerk said bluntly.

Preacher Swann stopped the bickering pair abruptly as he held up a hand for silence. They all stared at him with puzzled looks on their faces.

'Did anybody hear a noise?' he asked.

'What sort of noise?' The mayor looked round the room.

'I don't know, but it seemed to come from behind that desk.'

They all levelled their guns at the large piece of furniture as they approached it cautiously. Some of them gasped audibly as a frightened face appeared over the top of it. Fred Stales had not been able to flee the scene.

FIFTEEN

Jim Clark opened up the jailhouse early and admitted the aproned waiter from the hotel. The man bore a tray with some bacon, bread, and a pot of coffee for the prisoner who sat miserably in his cell.

Fred Stales had reason to be miserable. He had been there two days and was in for a hanging offence. With feeling in the town rising to a fever pitch as the story got around, he would be lucky not to be dragged out and lynched.

Marshal Clark had found the rig out on the trail. There were four dead men who had to be buried where they lay, much to the annoyance of the mortician. The marshal's return to town was greeted with news of the attack on the bank and the escape of three of the bandits. Nobody was feeling friendly towards the bank clerk who had been the cause of all the trouble.

An angry mob had gathered outside the jail-

146

house the evening Fred Stales was locked up by the mayor and the preacher. It had taken all Richard Swann's persuasive powers to stop a hanging then and there. Mayor Bradley was relieved when Jim Clark returned and took charge of the situation.

The marshal served the food to the prisoner and then went to sit at his desk to bring his paper work up to date. Nobody ever read it and the previous marshal's handwriting was not even legible. But that was the official routine.

'Marshal.'

Jim was a little surprised to hear the voice calling from the cell behind him. Fred Stales had been very quiet since his arrest. He was clearly terrified of the future. The lawman got up and went over to the bars.

'What is it, Fred?' he asked. 'Coffee too cold?'

'Marshal, they're gonna hang me, ain't they?' The little man's voice was trembling.

'You can bet on that. If the judge don't do it, the folk in Bluff Point sure as hell will. I can't hold them off for ever.'

'Could we make a deal?'

Jim tried to keep the surprise out of his voice.

'What sort of deal?' he asked quietly.

'Well, the Granton boys got away with about fifteen thousand dollars, I reckon. Suppose I can get it back for you?'

'How?' The marshal's voice was suddenly tense.

147

'I've gotta have a deal. Oh, I ain't askin' you to let me go completely. I know that ain't possible. But a lesser sentence. A spell in the county jail perhaps. Maybe even a pardon for helpin' the law. Could that be arranged?'

'I'd have to talk to the mayor and the judge. And you'd have to offer somethin' mighty solid.'

'I figure I can. The Grantons left me behind, so I owe them nothing. And I'd want that preacher fella here to be a witness. I'd trust him before any politico or lawyer. You get him, the mayor, and the judge in here, and I'll put you in the way of recoverin' the money and grabbin' the Granton gang.'

It was late afternoon when Mayor Bradley, Judge Lawson, Preacher Swann and the marshal all stood in front of the cell where Fred Stales clutched the bars with veined, clawlike hands.

They talked for a while of a deal that would let the little man off as lightly as possible. The judge was reluctant at first but with a true legal mind where money was concerned, agreed that lesser charges could be brought. Fred Stales was eventually persuaded to start talking.

'When I went to see the Grantons in their hideout,' he said, 'they insisted I come here with them. The bastards didn't trust me.'

'I am surprised,' the mayor said with a slight smile.

148

'I'm not a gunslinger but I had no choice, and they said they was goin' to take me with them to their new hideout. They didn't tell me where it was, but I reckon to know.'

He paused for effect and they all leaned forward eagerly.

'I heard them whisperin' about a cabin that some old woman has up near Mason's Creek.'

'Ma Henderson.' The preacher breathed the words in a shocked voice. 'She's a poor old woman with only a backward son to help her with the hogs and a milk cow.'

The mayor nodded. 'I know who you mean. Comes into town once or twice a year to sell a few sides of cured ham. She's only ten miles away and we can be there by mornin' with a posse.'

Fred Stales nodded eagerly. 'That's where you'll find them,' he said, 'and I reckon they didn't intend me to go there with 'em. I figure as how I'd have ended up dead once they had the money.'

'Likely you would,' the judge muttered as he breathed whiskey fumes all over the prisoner. 'Any sensible mortician would surely like havin' a fella like you on his waitin' list.'

The mayor drew Jim Clark aside.

'You think he's tellin' the truth?' he asked.

'Yeah, it's his only way out. I'll get a posse together and ride out there, but I'll have to have someone with me who knows where this place is.'

'I'll join you,' Preacher Swann said. 'The old lady may need a little help after such a frightening experience. And she does know me.'

'I'd sure appreciate that, Preacher,' Jim said thankfully.

'What about me?' Fred Stales rattled the bars to attract attention back to his plight.

'If things work out,' said the mayor, 'Judge Lawson will see you get treated right. And the preacher is here to make sure we keep our promise. You can't ask fairer than that, fella.'

'But what happens to me while the marshal's outa town? These folks could start thinkin' of a lynchin' party again.'

The mayor nodded happily. 'They sure as hell could.'

He looked at the judge and the preacher and then ushered them to the door.

'I want to thank you both for your trouble,' he said in his official voice, 'and you'll need to get yourself ready for this posse, Reverend. I'll just have a word with Jim here before he sets off. After all, we can't risk Fred bein' swung up on a loadin' beam, can we?'

When they were both safely away, Mayor Bradley turned his attention back to the prisoner.

'Now, lookit, Fred,' he said earnestly, 'you're gettin' on in life and I figure as how a spell in the county jail wouldn't do you any good at all. Here's what I suggest, if Jim agrees. You go with the posse, and that way we'll know you're levellin' with us. You'll also be safe from the folk here in town. If everythin' works out, you can get yourself lost on the way back. Nobody will be interested in huntin' you down once the money is safe and sound.'

Fred Stales nodded eagerly. 'I appreciate that, Mr Mayor,' he said thankfully.

'I thought you might, Fred. That alright with you, Marshal?'

The mayor stared hard at the lawman and Jim Clark nodded silently. He trusted nobody. The mayor least of all. When he was seeing Jess Bradley off the premises he queried the decision.

'Now, Jim,' the First Citizen said smoothly, 'once we get the cash, we have to keep our promise to that slimy sidewinder. A trial would cost money, and the councilmen don't like spendin' on anybody but themselves. We can afford to let him make a run for it. On the other hand, if he's given us a wrong steer, I figure as how your posse might just find a tree somewhere handy. See what I mean?'

Jim Clark saw what he meant and went to saddle the horses.

They set off an hour or so later, a group of seven men in whom the young marshal had little confidence. It had been difficult enough to get volunteers, and two of the posse were town drunks only joining him for the money, while another young fellow was trying to impress the local girls with his daring. None of the more solid citizens went along. They were all too busy earning a living and happy to leave the dirty work to others.

The posse stopped for the night near a brackish pool of water which only the horses would drink. They set off early the next morning to complete the last few miles before the sun became too hot. The preacher led the way, having made the trip several times to visit the old lady who farmed the few acres of fertile land with the help of her son. Richard Swann was the only man in the posse in whom Jim could place any real reliance, and he was not a fighter. He could shoot and had courage, but a preacher of the Gospel was not quite the same as an experienced lawman in an emergency.

Richward Swann slowed down as they reached a small stand of sycamores, which they would have to skirt.

'The cabin's on the far side,' he said. 'If we dismount here and go through the trees, we can take them by surprise. We'll have shelter and can command a clear view of the cabin. We'll have to be careful if there's any shooting. I don't want to see Ma Henderson and her boy hurt.'

Jim nodded agreement. He felt the same way but was not sure how to tackle the problem. The men got down from their horses and moved quietly through the trees towards the area of open ground where the small cabin lay beside a creek that flowed noisily enough for them to hear it from where they crouched in the undergrowth.

There was smoke coming from the iron chimney at one end of the log-built structure. They could see horses in a nearby corral while hogs snuffled around among a few hens and a tethered goat. There were no human beings to be seen but voices could be heard from the cabin. They waited for several minutes before the door of the building opened and a woman emerged.

'Is that Ma Henderson?' Jim asked the preacher.

'No, I've never seen her before.'

Fred Stales touched the marshal's arm.

'It's Ma Granton,' he whispered. 'Y'see, I steered you well, Marshal. They're here.'

'You did all right, fella. Now keep your head down.'

They watched the woman cross to a heap of cut wood and gather up an armful for the stove. She stood for a moment, looking around as though she sensed or heard something. Then she went back inside and shut the door.

Jim Clark motioned to the others to stay where they were while he crawled nearer to the corral to count the number of animals it contained. There were four horses and a mule that munched peacefully away on a good supply of fodder. Several saddles hung on the fence and one of them was a side-saddle which Jim guessed would belong to Ma Granton. He thought of releasing the mounts but it would be too noisy and the resultant shooting could endanger the lives of the Hendersons.

He crawled back to the others and told the preacher what he had seen.

'That'd be right,' Richard Swann agreed. 'Ma Henderson uses an old mule to get into town. Her son doesn't ride. She reckons that the mule has more sense than he has. What are we goin' to do, Jim?'

The lawman did not answer and tried to look as if he was giving the matter deep thought. The truth was that he wanted to rush in with guns blazing. Then he saw a possible way out.

Ma Granton had put some wood on the stove and the iron pipe breathed forth a plume of dark smoke that went straight up into the still air. Jim motioned his posse to gather a little closer.

'I'm gonna block that stovepipe,' he said tersely, 'and them folks is gonna come outa there needin' some fresh air. You take careful aim, and avoid Ma Henderson and her son. The preacher knows which they are, so you follow his orders. And while you're at it, don't put a bullet in my ass. Understand?'

They all grinned as they nodded their heads.

Jim crawled away to the left, keeping parallel with the cabin and just screened by the last of the trees. He came level with the side of the building and could see the roughly built wall with the pipe coming out and breathing dark smoke. He looked around desperately for something to climb on but nothing seemed to be handy.

He had been hoping there might be a rain barrel or some piece of fencing, but there did not appear to be anything that would help reach the low roof. He was almost going to give up and go back to the others when someone touched him on the shoulder. He almost jumped in fright and turned to find one of the town drunks grinning at him.

'I reckon as how you need a broad back to stand on, Marshal,' the man said quietly.

'I sure as hell do. Thanks, Steve.'

The two men crept forward, hoping that they were out of sight unless somebody actually put his head out of the small window. Steve knelt down on all fours and the marshal climbed on his sturdy back and found that his hands could easily reach the edge of the roof. He took a firm grip and hoisted himself up. His feet found purchase on the rough logs that made up the wall.

Most of the roof was of turf laid over planks. A variety of plants were growing vigorously. Jim was able to stand up as he took off his waistcoat, removed the items from the pockets, and then stuffed the garment into the stovepipe.

He stayed on the roof and drew his gun while Steve crawled back among the trees to join the others. Nothing happened for a minute or so and then a sort of pandemonium broke loose. The door of the cabin burst open and Alf Granton came out, swearing at his wife for putting wet wood on the stove. She followed him cursing as energetically that the wood was dry. Tom and Phil followed them with a little less fuss and the family stood arguing while Jim Clark looked down from the roof.

Richard Swann held back the guns of the posse while he checked for the Henderson family. They did not appear and he breathed a sigh of relief as he gave the order to fire.

The shots rang out as a deafening crescendo in the confined area. Alf Granton reeled back against his wife, his left arm shattered and useless. He was still able to draw the gun at his belt and he fired wildly into the trees. Ma Granton ran back into the cabin while her two sons were on their knees, both injured but still able to fight. Phil had been caught in the face and chest by the blast of a shotgun. He was peppered but the range had been too great to do fatal damage. He also drew his gun and was firing at the shrouded figures among the trees.

Tom was slower to take in the situation. He had

received a shotgun blast in both legs and a bullet had raked the side of his head. He started to draw his pistol and then changed his mind. He decided to crawl back to the cabin, only to be met by his mother who came storming out with a shotgun. She ignored his pleas for help and fired both barrels at the hidden posse. She reloaded with perfect calm and blasted away again.

It was Richard Swann who took her out of the fight. He aimed his Winchester carefully and the shot hit the butt of the gun as she broke it open for another load of cartridges. It fell from her hands and the posse could hear her vivid cursing above the noise of the shooting.

She hitched up her skirt and ran across to the corral to throw open the gate. Before anybody could stop her, she had seized the headband of one of the horses, mounted the animal, and was careering off to safer parts. None of the posse really felt like shooting at a woman, and Ma Granton escaped without an injury.

Alf had emptied his pistol and could not reload without the use of his injured left arm. He shoved the gun back in its holster and decided to follow in the footsteps of his wife. Another shot caught him in the leg as he reached the corral. He staggered for a moment but managed to grab one of the panicky mounts. He had difficulty getting on its back with only one usable hand, but he did manage it despite another blast from a shotgun as he sallied from the corral.

Tom and Phil were in the doorway of the cabin. A few more steps would take them safely behind the thick wooden walls and they would be able to hold out or use the Hendersons as hostages. The members of the posse seemed to realize that and all the guns blasted across the open space in a shattering volley. Both brothers collapsed against the thick wooden door and the world went silent again.

Jim Clark heaved himself down from the roof. He had not fired a shot but his work had brought about the results that were needed. His colleagues came slowly out from the tree-line, hardly believing how brave they had been and what stories they would have to tell back home.

Richard Swann entered the cabin, concerned only for the safety of the Henderson family. They were both tied to chairs and were coughing with the smoke that filled the little space.

Jim Clark followed the preacher into the neat place that had been a peaceful home to Ma Henderson and her boy. He was glad to see that the freed woman was full of spirit and none the worse for her experience. Her son, a hefty man in his twenties, even seemed to have enjoyed all the excitement. His childlike face was alight with his experience and he grinned welcomingly at the members of the posse.

Somebody climbed up on the roof to recover the marshal's waistcoat. It was somewhat the worse for wear but Ma Henderson promised to wash it after she had made them all some coffee and fried them a meal.

'Anybody hurt?' asked Jim as he looked round at the group of cheerful faces that crowded into the cabin.

'I reckon Fred Stales took one in the head,' somebody said with a broad wink. Jim looked hard at the men around him and sensed that they knew more than they were telling. He and the preacher went out to where the bank clerk lay among the trees. He had been shot in the back of the head at close range. Richard Swann's lips moved silently in prayer, and Jim felt that his triumph had suddenly turned sour.

The bank money lay on the table in two linen bags. They all stood around it and the eyes of the posse were wide and greedy as they stared at more money than they could ever hope to see again.

'We still have to chase after the two who escaped,' Jim said quietly. 'It's not goin' to be a long journey. One's wounded and they've got no saddles. This money had better go straight back to town. We can't go draggin' it all over the territory.'

He looked round at the hungry faces which still stared fixedly at the bags. The greed in their eyes was almost touchable. If they had time to think things over or to talk among themselves, he and the preacher would be likely to end up dead. He nodded to Richard Swann.

'I reckon as how that's your job, Preacher,' he said firmly. 'Take the cash back to town and tell the mayor that the Hendersons are safe and we're after the last of the Granton gang. Now, let's have this coffee and be about our business.'

They set out some twenty minutes later, the posse moving north and Preacher Swann heading south. The bags were strapped to his saddle and he felt wearily pleased at the part he had played. His stout wife and three children would be proud of him when he got home. He stopped after a while to let his horse chew on some sweet grass. He thought of his town and the family he had, and of all the things that had happened in his life.

Then he made up his mind and did what he had done once before when he was carrying a large sum of money. He decided to make a fresh start. He turned his mount towards the east.